It was hot.

"Damn it," Chance growled, ~~~~~~~~~ her as if she had the plague. *"Damn it."*

"What..." Ally had to clear her throat to speak. "What was that about?"

"Nothing. It was just a kiss."

That had been *just a kiss?*

Well, she was certainly glad he'd cleared that up for her, because she'd been quite positive it had been more, far more, as in something from the heart, from the soul.

"I meant to stay away from you," Chance said.

"Well, you're not doing a very good job."

"I'm going to try harder."

"Good. Because..." Ally's throat tightened. She wanted him, plain and simple. And he wanted her, too, she knew that. But he didn't *want* to want her, and that hurt. Suddenly she missed her own quiet world. "I want my old life back," she whispered.

He nodded curtly. "Then go get it."

So simple. So why did it seem so hard?

Dear Reader,

There's nothing more sexy than a hero who knows his own mind and isn't afraid to speak it. T. J. Chance is definitely one of those men: confident, gorgeous, not to mention ready, able and willing.

Ally Wheeler admires these qualities, and though she's naturally not superconfident herself, nor ready, able and willing, she's hoping to learn. From Chance.

Only, Chance doesn't want to teach Ally to walk on the wild side. He doesn't want to do anything with her, especially fall in love, which is exactly what happens. Hope you enjoy this last installment of the MEN OF CHANCE miniseries!

Jill Shalvis

P.S. You can write to me c/o Harlequin, 225 Duncan Mill Road, Don Mills, Ontario, M3B 3K9, Canada.

Books by Jill Shalvis

HARLEQUIN TEMPTATION
742—WHO'S THE BOSS?
771—THE BACHELOR'S BED
804—OUT OF THE BLUE

CHANCE ENCOUNTER
Jill Shalvis

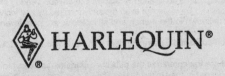

HARLEQUIN®

TORONTO • NEW YORK • LONDON
AMSTERDAM • PARIS • SYDNEY • HAMBURG
STOCKHOLM • ATHENS • TOKYO • MILAN • MADRID
PRAGUE • WARSAW • BUDAPEST • AUCKLAND

To my own man of Chance, David.

ISBN 0-373-25922-0

CHANCE ENCOUNTER

Copyright © 2001 by Jill Shalvis.

This edition published by arrangement with Harlequin Books S.A.

® and TM are trademarks of the publisher. Trademarks indicated with
® are registered in the United States Patent and Trademark Office, the
Canadian Trade Marks Office and in other countries.

Visit us at www.eHarlequin.com

Printed in U.S.A.

"YOU'RE FIRED."

"*What?*" Ally meant to sound fierce but she might as well have been a squeaky mouse. "You...can't do that."

"Oh, yes, I can." Professor Langley Weatherby III, every bit the antiquated snob his name suggested, peered over his small wire-rimmed spectacles. "You're no longer a librarian at this university, Ms. Wheeler. Consider yourself officially unemployed."

"But—" Ally *loved* her work, loved everything about it, the feel of the glorious old books in her hands, the scent of aging paper, the pleasure of helping students soak up all that knowledge.

And the silence, most of all she loved the silence.

"We'll give you two weeks' severance pay," the professor said. "More than generous, given the scandal."

Ah, yes, the scandal. Not that anyone had let her forget it for one moment. It hadn't been her fault, and feeling her throat burn, she swiped at the moisture in her eyes, as if flicking away a pesky piece of lint instead of her hopes and dreams.

The professor let out a heavy sigh and thrust a handkerchief beneath her nose. "You do see our position," he said gruffly, but with slightly less antagonism. "We can't let you stay now."

It was hard to believe that little Miss Goody-Two-shoes had gotten herself into so much trouble. First with the professor, then the head of the school himself, and finally, when no one had believed Ally's story, with the authorities. She'd even had an eventful ride to the San Francisco police station for questioning, an experience that would surely headline her nightmares for the rest of her life.

Ironic, since in all of her nearly twenty-six years she'd never so much as been sent to the principal's office. "But Thomas was the one who stole the classics," she said for at least the hundredth time.

"They were *priceless* first edition literary classics that had been at our university for decades, Ms. Wheeler. Your boyfriend used your special clearance to steal them."

But what would she do without her job? Her heart and soul were embedded in these brick walls, because here she wasn't mousy Ally. Here she was important. She belonged.

"This decision is final."

She wouldn't beg. With her stomach somewhere near the vicinity of her feet, she stood, lifted her chin to the level of the professor's aristocratic nose, and walked out of her beloved library for the last time. She passed the biology building, the Social Studies Hall and the Student Union before moving toward the park, her second favorite place on earth. Here was where she left her car every morning, so at the end of a day filled with books, she could unwind by feeding the squirrels.

Fired. Fired. *Fired.* The word rang in her head.

Well, if being let go was the worst thing to ever happen to her, then so be it. So she'd been forced to leave the best job she'd ever had. She'd survive. Probably.

But where was her car? Craning her neck, she looked to the right, then to the left— *Oh, no.*

Had she really thought her day couldn't get worse?

Her fifteen-year-old tomato-red Escort coupe, temperamental and spunky at the best of times—of which this wasn't—was gone all right. It had rolled down the steep hill.

And smashed into a plush, very new-looking BMW sports car.

HER ANSWERING MACHINE had just clicked on when Ally wearily made her way into her apartment.

"Ally?" came a cranky, smoke-ladened voice. "I know you're there, pick up the phone this instant!"

"I don't think so," she said, grateful to have avoided Mrs. Snipps, landlady from hell.

"Listen missy, I sold the building."

Ally dropped her purse and stared at the machine.

"I'm retiring to the Bahamas."

Ally sank to her couch.

"And you have until next month to get out," the cragly voice continued. "*Six weeks.* Don't cause me any trouble, girl."

At the sound of the dial tone, Ally let out a choked laugh. "Trouble?" she muttered. "It's only my middle name." She was jobless, and now soon to be homeless as well. Not to mention the major dent her car had put into that brand-spanking-new BMW. She had insurance, but she also had a very high deductible that might as well be a million dollars for all her ability to pay it.

Another mirthless laugh escaped. Her life was not only over, it was pitiful.

The phone rang again.

What now? Dammit, she was tired. Tired of jumping at the sound of the telephone, tired of being insecure and mousy all the time. Suddenly mad, she straightened on the couch.

No more doormat, she decided as she yanked up the receiver. "Hello!" And because being forceful felt so good, she added, *"Who is this and what do you want?"*

"It's Thomas."

At the sound of the confident masculine voice, her nearly nonexistent temper exploded. How dare he call after destroying her life. "You! You— You big jerk!" Oh great. Was "you big jerk" the biggest insult she could come up with?

"Listen, Ally," he said quickly. A strange clinking sound came over the phone. "I need you to get me a lawyer. Like yesterday."

What had she seen in this guy?

But she already knew the answer to that, painful as it was to admit. He was a gorgeous, smooth, elegant man who'd noticed her. Unlike everyone else in her life, he hadn't needed her money—little as there was—he hadn't required her mothering skills, hadn't wanted anything from her except...her. More than that, he'd given her attention.

How pathetic was that? He'd made plain Ally Wheeler—of average height, average weight, average hair and eyes—feel beautiful.

It'd taken awhile for the stars to clear from her eyes. Only then had she been able to see Thomas for the user and con man that he was, though not in time to save her job, or the library's classics.

"No, I won't get you a lawyer," she said, winding up to let loose some of her pent-up feelings. "And another thing—"

"Officer Daniel here," a strange voice said in her ear. "Time's up."

Ally stared at the phone and for the first time in days let out a genuine laugh. Thomas had called from jail, in handcuffs if the clanking noise meant anything. Wasn't life just one big excitement after another?

NO JOB CAME THROUGH. Thanks to the ruthless rumors about Ally's involvement with the priceless missing volumes, no library in the entire state would touch her. And nothing could soften the cold, hard facts. She had little to no savings, three sisters in college counting on her financial help, elderly parents on a fixed income, and she was staring poverty in the face.

She needed a job, any job. Without one, who would rent her a place to live? Her sisters were all settled in dorms. Her parents, who'd had their kids late in life, lived in a senior center. She had no one to turn to.

It was then that the letter came. Lucy was Ally's mother's second cousin by marriage, and though they didn't get to see each other often, they corresponded regularly. Lucy's weekly letters from Wyoming, where she ran a mountain resort, were always the exciting highlight of Ally's day. Just a month ago, there'd been a terrible fire, and Lucy had been crushed at the loss of over one hundred acres of lush landscape. They'd written each other frequently since then, with Ally doing her best to cheer up Lucy.

Unlike the others though, this letter turned Ally's life completely around. Or upside down, depending on how one looked at it.

Dearest Ally,
    You won't believe this, but I've broken my hip and ankle, and landed myself in the hospital for a while. Blast those newfangled mountain bikes!

Ally blinked. The sixty-something Lucy on a mountain bike?

    We're desperately racing to clean up from the fire before our summer season can start. We need that acreage cleared for our mountain bikers and hikers, or I'll lose business.
    So I need a favor, Ally, a big one. Come stay at the resort while I'm in the hospital recovering from this stupid mishap. I have a great staff, but there's nothing like family to watch out for your interests. You've got good business experience,

and a degree. You'll make a great general manager.

General manager? Ally shuddered, her head filled with visions of huge snowdrifts. Endless dark, haunting forests.

Big bugs.

I've arranged for you to be on the payroll, so take a leave of absence from that boring, stagnant, indoor job and you'll never regret it. Give me a month of your time, that's all. Do it for me. Do it because I'm desperate and need you.

Do it for yourself.

Love, Lucy

From the envelope fell a plane ticket dated two days from now. Ally sat there staring down at it, her eyes glued to the date.

She couldn't have just been offered a miracle, could she? She couldn't really be sitting here holding a one way ticket out of the disaster her life had become. To say she was afraid was the understatement of the century. She had less than a hundred dollars left in her checking account, no car and no job.

But...Wyoming?

The normally quiet and unassuming Ally would never consider such a thing, but that woman was gone, replaced by a woman determined to stop helping everyone else and help herself for a change. And maybe even enjoy herself while she was at it.

She supposed she could say Lucy needed her, that her family did as well. That by going she'd be fulfilling just another family obligation. But those thoughts irritated her. Her *entire* life had been dictated by the needs of others. No more.

So she'd hit rock bottom. It meant she had nowhere to go but up, right? And she wanted *more* than just survival, she wanted to succeed at something. Anything. For once she wanted to be great at her life. She was going to go Wyoming. *Look out big bugs*, she thought. *Here I come.*

2

TWO DAYS LATER, Ally stepped off the plane and stared at the wide, open sky and outlying sharp, majestic mountains, completely awestruck. It all seemed so...big.

As she walked across the tarmac, the wind hit her, a stinging, sharp draft that nearly knocked her sideways. "You're not in Kansas anymore, Dorothy," she whispered, glancing at the threatening, thunderous clouds gathering on the horizon.

No problem. This was going to be fun. She had to repeat that to herself when a pesky little voice inside her head kept saying, *I want my quiet, cozy life back.*

Her old life was gone for now. This is what she had. With a lifted chin and a swagger that was mostly bravado, she continued away from the plane toward the small terminal. She'd just retrieve her luggage, find a cab and go meet Lucy at the hospital, where they could spend a little time catching up. Then she'd head over to the resort and meet the staff Lucy had described as a young, capable, tight unit.

She was ready! She was going to dig in and help with the fire clean-up. She was going to try everything and anything, and succeed no matter what. No more taking care of everyone. No more putting everyone else first.

It was Ally Wheeler's turn.

She staggered a bit, pummeled by the increasing wind. The other passengers, who'd seemed so cityish on the plane, suddenly all had sweaters or jackets out. Several of the men had placed cowboy hats on their heads, and she noted for the first time, they all wore boots.

She felt like a fish out of water, especially when her cell phone rang.

"Ally!"

Pesky younger sister number one. "You're already gone," wailed Dani. "I didn't get to talk to you before you left. What if I need you?"

Only calmness worked on Dani, and Ally strove for some now as she was pelted by the wind, jostled by people walking past her, and all around overwhelmed by her new surroundings. "I told you I was going." It was the most soothing voice she could muster. "And if you need me, Dani, you can do as you're doing right now and call."

"But what if I need money?"

For the first time, Ally couldn't find any patience for her baby sister. "You might try putting in a few hours of work." She was nearly at the terminal now and her mind was far from home. Her heart was racing as she walked toward this new adventure of hers. "I've got to go, okay? I'll call you later."

"But—"

Ally disconnected, and forced herself to let go of the

guilt. She was no longer saving the world, she was living for herself for a change. It was exciting. Scary. Her hair whipped at her face. Her blouse, perfectly suitable for May in San Francisco, plastered itself to her body, providing no barrier against the chill, but she kept moving.

And then found her gaze locked with a stranger's.

His wide shoulders were propping up the wall of the terminal, one long leg bent, foot braced on the brick behind him. He wore reflective sunglasses and a crooked, *follow-this* smile.

He tugged off the glasses and suddenly his pose didn't seem lazy but...coiled. He was looking right at her, *through* her, with dark, dark, piercing eyes.

Feeling silly, and too skittish for someone who was supposed to be tough instead of wussy, Ally forced herself to remain calm. She knew she was cold, knew too, that it was painfully obvious through the blouse she wore, the one that at this very moment was plastered to her like a second skin, outlining her every curve for his inspection.

And inspect he did, slowly, thoroughly, leaving her blushing from toes to roots. Out of necessity she continued to move toward him, her one and only goal at this point to get warm. Closer now, she could see his eyes were blue; the clear, startling dark blue of the ocean deep. His hair was sun-kissed blond, on the wrong side of long, hitting past his collar at the back of his neck. No razor had touched his skin in at least two days, and the stubble only emphasized his firm, tough mouth. His faded jeans, leather bomber jacket and attitude assured her he was the poster boy for *bad*.

"Excuse me," he said, facing her fully. He was tall, and built like a man who used his body often. A gold hoop shone at his ear. His face was rugged, tanned and comfortably lived in, holding the sweet, saintly expression of an angel—with the devastating, irresistible smile of the devil. But it was his low, husky voice that grabbed her, a voice that was so innately...*sexy* she felt all her X chromosomes jerk to attention.

"Ms. Wheeler, right?" He lifted one dark blond brow and shifted that tall, leanly muscled frame, drawing her attention to the way his Levi's caressed his lower body, but she couldn't concentrate on that at the moment.

Because he knew her name.

That couldn't be good, or safe. She wanted to be cool but the little mouse resurfaced. And he looked like he ate little mice for breakfast. "Who are you?"

He gave her a pleasant enough smile while he studied her. Pleasant being relative of course, in a face that could tempt the gods. "I'm T. J. Chance. Lucy sent me for you."

"She didn't have to do that, I can catch a cab to the hospital."

He chuckled, a deep rumbling sound that did funny things to her belly, even though that laughter was clearly directed at her.

"They don't have cabs in Wyoming?" she asked, a little defensively.

"Sure." He lifted a broad shoulder. "But even if you managed to get one, it'd cost you about a hundred bucks to go that far."

A hundred dollars. More than she had. Her shoulders slumped. "A bus then?"

"No such luck. But don't worry. I'm not as bad as they say." A wicked gleam came into his eyes. "Not quite."

Who was he kidding? He looked bad to the bone, a fact that was both oddly thrilling and disturbing at the same time.

She wanted to be bad to the bone, just once. "Look, Mr. Chance—"

"Just Chance."

"Chance," she corrected cautiously. "It's nothing personal, really, it's just—" That she'd sworn off men, *especially* men like him, men who could make her every nerve sizzle by just standing there. "I don't take rides from strangers."

"Ah. Spoken like a true city girl."

"Well, I *am* a city girl."

"I'd never have noticed," he said wryly, taking in her wispy sandals, her lightweight khakis, her even more lightweight blouse. "And we're not strangers. Lucy is more like my family than..." Something flickered in his deep, unreadable gaze. "Well, my family." He stepped close, so close he blocked out the bright sunshine with his big, rugged body.

Ally barely came up to his chin and she backed away, because learning to be tough didn't mean she had to be stupid.

"Hey, relax." He lifted his hands in innocence, but somehow she doubted he'd ever been innocent. "You're turning blue is all."

"That's because I'm freezing."

"Should have brought a jacket." He looked very nice and toasty in his. He slipped his hands in the pockets. The leather crinkled enticingly, looking luxuriously warm, and in envy, her entire body leaned toward it.

Chance's eyes narrowed.

"Don't worry. I wouldn't ask you to share." But then she shivered again, and with a disgusted look, he yanked the leather off, leaving him in a soft-looking, black T-shirt.

"Here, dammit." His arms were as tanned and rugged as his face, and roped with strength. When he held out the jacket, she caught a glimpse of a small tattoo where his sleeve was stretched taut over his biceps.

Bad to the bone, she thought again. "I couldn't."

"Now you're being stubborn." He set the jacket on her shoulders, enveloping her in his lingering body heat and outdoorsy, very male scent. For a second, his hands skimmed over her shoulders, then he slipped them into the pockets of his jeans, legs spread wide on the ground, sure and confident in a way Ally reluctantly had to admire. He was everything *she* wanted to be, here in Wildland, U.S.A.

"A thin blouse isn't the smartest thing to be wearing in the mountains," he noted. "It could still snow. You'll need to be more prepared."

She wondered how prepared *he'd* be in *her* world. But the truth was, T. J. Chance looked pretty darn capable. Without a doubt, he'd fit in anywhere, he'd make sure of it.

And suddenly her newfound and not quite secure baby-new strength deserted her. For a terrible moment, it all seemed so completely overwhelming. The loss of her job, her apartment, her quiet, happy life...and now this too rugged, too masculine, too everything man was looking at her as if she was an idiot.

Well she *was* an idiot. She'd lost her job, her apartment. She'd lost her dignity and all self-confidence.

"Ah hell," he said, going very still as he looked at her. "You're not over there crying, are you?"

Ally got busy trying to suck it all up, trying to be the tough girl she wanted to be, but he looked so fierce with all that bad attitude blazing from his eyes, that the harder she tried, the more her eyes stung from the effort.

"Perfect." He sounded so annoyed, that a laugh shot out of her, which had a tear escaping down her frozen cheek.

He pointed at her. "Stop it."

Of course she couldn't, and he slapped at his pockets, muttering beneath his breath as he thrust a napkin under her nose, reminding her of the incident with the professor.

His handkerchief had been soft cotton, laundered and pressed.

This napkin was rough and rumpled paper.

"Take it," he demanded roughly. "Take it and

knock off the waterworks. They don't work on me." Before she could take the proffered napkin, he grabbed her arm and led her through the terminal, stopping inside to once again shove the napkin at her. "Your nose is running."

Perfect. She swiped at it and gave Mr. Rough and Tumble a sideways look. He seemed unraveled, and she found it...amusing. He was insensitive. In a hurry. He was edgy and quite likely to be horrible to work with. And tears scared him. It made her want to smile for some silly reason. She sniffed loudly, relieved to be on the edge of good humor again instead of the mortifying tears.

"I'll go get the Jeep," he told her. "You stay here and just...stay here." He backed away as if she had the plague.

Odd how much better that made her feel, scaring the scariest of them all.

"I'll be gone only a minute." He narrowed his eyes. "Don't do anything stupid."

"Don't worry." She blew her nose again. "I've filled my stupid quota for the next few moments at least."

He looked at her as if he thought maybe she'd lost her mind. And she most definitely had, because suddenly, she couldn't wait to get started with the rest of her life. She zipped up his big, soft jacket and snuggled deep into the warmth. It smelled like citrus soap and one-hundred-percent man, and because it was so delicious, she inhaled deeply.

Then, because she felt good and ready, she also took his ride.

CITY GIRL GOT herself together quickly, a fact that made Chance most grateful. God, he really hated the feeling that came over him when a woman cried. Frustrated. Stupid. *Guilty*, though it couldn't have possibly been his fault, not this time.

No way.

But there was no denying that Ally Wheeler reminded him of Tina. Though she'd been dead ten years now, just looking at Ally's slender frame, at her obvious naiveté, was a sharp, very unwelcome reminder of his past.

What had Lucy been thinking, bringing this woman here? It *had* to be some sort of misguided family loyalty. He wondered if either of his own two older brothers would feel that same family loyalty if he needed something.

Yeah, he had to admit, they would. No matter that the three of them rarely saw eye to eye on anything, that they didn't understand each other, they'd come through.

"Th-think we can have the heat on?"

He glanced at his temporary boss. She was huddled on the seat of his Jeep, her arms wrapped tight around her middle, her lips still a most interesting shade of blue, even as her chin was jutted up in the air. Hey maybe she'd get so cold she'd want to go home. He cheered up at the thought. "It's warm enough in here," he told her.

She leaned forward and turned on the heater herself, sighing with pleasure when the hot air hit her legs.

He shook his head and concentrated on the road. "You'll hate winter."

"Don't worry. I won't be here that long." Her teeth were chattering. "N—not that it's your concern."

Only a woman could go from vulnerable to annoying so quickly. "*Everything* you do while you're here is my concern." Which rankled. The last thing he wanted was to be responsible for a lightweight who got cold in sixty-degree weather.

She looked at him with wide eyes the amazing color of a stormy gray sky, and it made him narrow his own, realizing he'd only given her a cursory glance before. Her hair, a wild honey-colored mess from the wind, lay in tangles around her face. Her curvy body was an asset, in spite of her habit of hunching her shoulders, as if she was trying to disappear.

She wasn't his type. Nope, he liked a woman fast, earthy and as wild as the Wyoming landscape around him. Oh, and let's not forget overtly sexual. Yeah, someone who enjoyed her body and knew how to use it. Antsy Ally was none of that.

"Why is that?" she asked.

Chance had lost track of the conversation. He leisurely ran his gaze back up to her eyes. "Why what?"

Irritation flickered, and she crossed her arms tightly over her breasts, which only amused him, because now they plumped up nicely, giving him an even better view.

"Why am I your concern?" she repeated.

What was it Lucy had demanded of him? *Take good care of my Ally. Her safety and welfare are on your shoul-*

ders. Dammit. He promptly forgot about Ally's breasts and remembered his irritation. "Everything and everyone at Sierra Peak is my concern," he said curtly.

Her eyes went even wider. "You work at the resort?"

"I *am* the resort. I'm the mountain manager."

A sound that was little more than a squeak escaped her before she cleared her throat and tried again. "What exactly does a mountain manager do?"

"Besides report to the GM?" He downshifted to take a tight mountain curve and shrugged. "Anything and everything. I lead treks, plan expeditions. Petition land trusts for more property. Blaze new trails to lure world-class athletes from all over the world."

"All that?"

"I also set up all the competitive events."

"Oh."

"And both the ski patrol and our new biking patrol are under my command, as well as the rest of the staff."

"So...you do it all."

"Yup."

"And what do I do as GM?"

He grinned. "Manage me."

She stared at him with such horror he would have cracked up if she wasn't to be his boss, for all intents and purposes, until Lucy returned. To say he didn't appreciate authority was an understatement.

"So...you probably know how to ski and bike and do all that outdoor stuff really well, right?" she asked.

"Everyone on the staff is an accomplished athlete.

It's a requirement for employment." He took his gaze off the road and settled it on her. "Unless, of course, there's some sort of family deal."

She blushed and nibbled on her lower lip. "Lucy asked me to come."

He knew that, and had no idea why it bothered him so. Why *she* bothered him. "And now I'm a baby-sitter."

Her eyes flashed at that. "I don't need a baby-sitter."

"Good. I don't want to be one."

"Well then, don't even think about it." What looked like years of frustration poured from her as she spoke. "For once I'm going to do what I want, when I want, without worrying about which sister has tuition or which other sister needs me to straighten out one of her messes." She used her hands when she talked, and he wondered if she used her hands like that during sex.

"I'm going to stop thinking about everyone else and think about myself for a change." She nodded sharply, as if reinforcing the decision. Her eyes glowed with passion. "I want to do as I please, *when* I please. If I want to go dancing barefoot in the grass, I will. If I want to go howl at the moon, I will. I'll go hog wild if I feel like it. Whatever comes my way, I'll do it." Then she lifted that stubborn chin and flashed pride out of her stormy gaze. "On my own."

All that fierceness, mixed in with her obvious naïveté, both terrified and aroused him. Which in turn annoyed the hell out of him. "Fine."

"Fine," she repeated, then fell silent through the next set of winding curves, which he liked. Silence was good.

And apparently she'd finally warmed up because she'd stopped hugging herself. Not that he cared that she'd been cold, but now all her nice curves were right there for his perusal, only inches away.

How did a prudish librarian end up with such a lush body anyway?

"Lucy probably finds herself bogged down with paperwork most of the time," she said eventually. "You know, from behind a desk, right?"

Lucy behind a desk? Not unless she was chained there. In their mutual running of the resort, he and Lucy had meshed perfectly. "Did she happen to mention *why* she's in the hospital?" he asked.

"Oh, yeah." She fell silent again, but for a shorter time, dammit. "You do a lot of dangerous stuff, then?"

He sighed, loud and long. "Are you going to talk all the way back?"

She blinked, and shut her mouth.

For one blessed moment.

"I guess I am going to talk all the way there," she said.

"Terrific," he muttered.

"So...do you find yourself living on the edge a lot out here?"

She thought bike riding was living on the edge? This was going to be one hell of a long haul. "Yep, we like our edge out here."

"Oh." She bit her lower lip. "Well, I've read about it."

Great. She'd read about it. He laughed.

She didn't. She looked resolutely ahead at the beautiful landscape. "Things are going to change here though," she said softly. "I can feel it."

"Is this about the going hog wild thing?"

"None of your business."

Oh, *now* she wanted to be private. "You're not under some misguided impression that you're going to change your lack of living on the edge while you're *here*, right?"

"Yep."

"Oh, no you don't."

"Oh no I don't what?"

He only groaned. "Just what I need. A walking, talking, *irritating* accident waiting to happen."

Her disbelief was clear. "Excuse me?"

"Not on my watch," he said firmly. *"No way."*

"Well I'm not on your 'watch,' so relax." She turned from him and once again looked out the window.

Oh yeah. Right. *Relax.* She didn't have a clue. He was short-staffed and exhausted from working around the clock since the fire. The fire that was now going to set back their summer season God only knew how long, and cost a ton of money that Sierra Peak Resort couldn't afford to lose.

And she wanted him to relax. Good luck. He loved his life here, he really did. His job fulfilled his serious sweet spot for thrill and excitement. His whole life had, ever since his father had first taken him to Tibet at the age of five, where they'd climbed mountains for three straight seasons.

In his own unorthodox way, his father had tried to instill a deep sense of wanderlust within each of his three sons, and the need to constantly push for bigger and better. Chance's two older brothers, Brandon and Kell, hadn't exactly embraced the family lifestyle. Like most others, they'd never understood the wanderlust, the inexplicable need to explore and seek adventure. As a result, they'd also never understood their father, or Chance. Both had rebelled against their unstructured and atypical childhoods, and gone in the opposite direction—straight into the military.

Not Chance. Blindly follow authority? Never. He relished his freedom and independence too much for that. As his father before him, Chance craved...well, adventure. Freedom. Not many understood the need. Certainly not a woman, though Tina had been the only one to come close to making him believe she had.

She'd been a kindergarten aide in Colorado when he'd come through on a skiing binge. They'd both been nineteen. Chance had skied his brains out by day and seduced Tina's brains out by night. She'd been so sweet, so fragile. Compassionate. Ridiculous as it had seemed, he'd been inexplicably drawn to her, and try as he might, he couldn't get her out of his system. When it had come time for Chance to move on, she'd wanted to come with him, but he couldn't see her living his wanderlust lifestyle. She'd insisted, tried to prove to him she could by going on a month long trek with her girlfriends. Within five days, just enough time for her to get good and deep into the wilderness in Canada, she'd fallen ill. By the time she'd gotten to a hospital, she'd had pneumonia.

She'd died there.

And though he'd told himself he hadn't loved her, his chest had felt as though it had caved in. Most of it had been guilt, but he had a terrible feeling it'd been more, much more.

Never again had he fallen for a sweet, little thing with huge, expressive eyes. Never again had he let a woman convince him he needed her for anything but a hot, lusty sexual release.

It'd been awhile since any sort of sexual release at all, thanks to his insane work schedule. Which had to explain why he was driving this annoying-as-hell woman—who just happened to have big, expressive eyes, damn her—and all he could think about was the way that her blouse had continued to cling her to her like a second skin.

Suddenly hot, he leaned forward and flicked off the heater, at the exact moment she leaned forward to crank it up. Their hands brushed, and when he looked at her, his mouth was only a fraction of an inch from hers.

Skittish, she jerked back, and he had to smile grimly. No hot, lusty sexual release coming from *that* corner.

Now she had her nose pressed to the window, watching the magnificent landscape go by, and he had to shake his head. "I'm guessing you've never been in the wilds before."

"Not unless you count the downtown bus station at about five o'clock in the afternoon."

"That's a zoo, not the wilds," he said, disgusted, and unable to help his curiosity, he asked, "You've never even camped?"

"Once." Her lips curved, and her eyes unfocused a little as she remembered. "In my backyard. I ate marshmallows, drank sodas and sang songs. It was wonderful. Then I was bit by a spider and it got infected, and I threw up the marshmallows. And then on the way to the bathroom, I slipped on the garden hose and broke my ankle." Her mouth twisted wryly. "Haven't camped since." She sighed. "Or eaten marshmallows." Then she bit her lip and slid him a glance. "And you should know, the last time I was on a bike I broke my arm. I was twelve. But I can swim, just not really well."

Amazing. *Terrifying.* "But certainly you've traveled around."

"No."

How could someone be so *content* as to stay in one place? It was beyond his comprehension. "So why did you come?"

"Because Lucy needed me."

"You always come running when people ask?"

Her nose went in the air. "It's called family loyalty."

He slowly shook his head. "No obligation would ever hold me to a place I didn't want to be."

"You sound bitter."

Nope. Just uninterested in any serious ties. There

was no payoff in getting his heart tromped on, as he knew all too well.

"And anyway," she said. "Who said I didn't want to be here?" But her shoulders slumped just a little. Her eyes filled with worry. "God. I hope I'm not a fool to think I can do this."

Just what he wanted to hear. *Sorry, Lucy,* he thought as he whipped the Jeep around, not quite managing to hide his relief.

Ally gripped the dash and stared at him, alarm etched on her features. "What are you doing?"

Getting as far from you as possible. "I'll take you back to the airport."

"No! You...you can't."

"You're a fool to think you can do this," he repeated, not very patiently or kindly. "You said it, not me."

"I know what I said," she snapped. Right in front of his eyes, she drew herself up, his leather jacket crinkling softly on her body.

And she suddenly didn't remind him of Tina at all.

"I was just thinking out loud," she said haughtily. "Don't listen to me."

Well, wasn't that a woman for you. "Don't listen to you. Is that your first order?"

She crossed her arms over her chest. Her stormy eyes blasted him. They should have been icy, but they weren't, not at all. The woman had quite the passionate streak.

He was certain she had no idea how much of a turn-on that was, or she'd undoubtedly stop immediately.

"Turn back around," she demanded.

"Why?"

"Because I'm here. I know I've been a little wishy-washy, but that's over now. I'm going for the adventure. Biking, skiing, whatever you can dish out here in Wyoming, bring it on. I'm letting loose."

The thought of her letting loose was the first terror he'd felt in a good long time. "Wait a minute—"

"No," she said quickly, pointing at him. "Don't talk. Don't reason. Don't—" Her gaze dropped, to his mouth, then further still, to his chest, and then below that for long enough to have his body leaping to hopeful attention. She jerked her face back up. Her cheeks pinkened. "Just..." She seemed to struggle for the right words for a moment, and Chance prepared himself to be blistered with a pithy comment.

"Just...*drive!*" she finished triumphantly, leaning back.

Oh, wasn't she fierce. He laughed.

She didn't so much as crack a smile, and once he realized he was truly good and stuck with her, he swallowed his mirth with little difficulty.

He prayed she came to her senses really soon. Or that she'd trip over another garden hose.

3

ALLY WALKED DOWN the hall toward Lucy's hospital room, butterflies attacking her stomach. Thankfully Chance had stayed in the waiting room. She couldn't concentrate on visiting with Lucy if he was in the room distracting her, and distract her he most definitely would. Even if he hadn't been so tall, dark and earth-stoppingly gorgeous, his take-me-as-I-am persona would have attracted her.

Attracted her. Dangerous stuff, made more so by the way just one look from him had her every nerve dancing. Had she learned nothing from her last relationship? Had she forgotten already? Pretty, dangerous men equaled heartache!

Her sandals echoed smartly on the white tile. The stark walls seemed to glare at her, trying to suck away her shaky, burgeoning confidence, so she simply walked faster, refusing to give in.

"Well, get on in here!" Lucy said when Ally stopped at her door. "Let me get a look at you." She was smiling, with long, wild auburn hair streaked with gray, sweet sparkling green eyes and the most impish smile Ally'd ever seen.

"This can't be the right room," Ally said, amazed. "I

was expecting suffering. No one looking as good as you could be suffering."

"Oh, I'm suffering!" Lucy assured her. "I can't even walk. Check this out."

Ally moved closer and saw Lucy did indeed have some sort of traction in place for her hip. "Ouch."

"You look like hell, did you know that?" Lucy opened her arms for a hug, which Ally gave her along with a wry laugh.

"Thanks ever so much."

Lucy just smiled serenely, and settled more comfortably. She poured both herself and Ally a cup of water from a pitcher by her bed. "Don't worry," she said, handing Ally a cup. "Wyoming will take care of you. I'm so glad you've come. You've met Chance? Isn't he sweet?"

Ally, who'd just taken a sip of water, nearly choked. "*Sweet?*" They couldn't be talking about the same man.

Lucy smiled and nodded. "I know. He's sweet and much, much more. Isn't he wonderful?"

Wonderful looking, maybe. But big, bad Chance was the last thing Ally wanted to discuss. "You still haven't said how you're feeling," she said, looking for a distraction here. "Are you in a lot of pain?"

"Ah," Lucy nodded sagely. "The old subject change. Nice one." Some of her joy seemed to fade. "So you hated him."

"No, of course not. I didn't...*hate* him."

Lucy sank back a bit into her pillows, dipping her chin down just enough so that she didn't quite meet

Ally's gaze. "Because I'd feel so badly if you were forced to work with someone you didn't like."

Like? No. Lust? *Oh yeah.* Bad combo. But for her new lease on life, she could work with him, could learn everything she needed to know from him, even if just looking at him in jeans and a T-shirt had set her hormones raging. "It'll be fine," she insisted. "We'll be fine."

"Really? Oh, honey, I'm so glad. It makes it so much easier for me since…well, considering my condition."

That sounded ominous. "Is something wrong with the way you're healing?"

"Oh, nothing a little time won't fix." Lucy played with the edge of her sheet, her bottom lip caught between her teeth. "I'm just so worried about the resort. The fire ruined everything, you know. Getting our summer season started is going to be a challenge. You'll stay, won't you, Ally?"

She grasped Lucy's cool, calloused hand. "Of course." She had a month before she had to get back to San Francisco to clear out her apartment. A month to figure out what she wanted to be when she grew up. "But quite frankly, Chance seems more than capable—"

"Oh, he's capable all right." Lucy laughed. "And with his good looks and easy smiles, he can convince any of the staff to do just about anything. But family is family."

Ally thought about Chance's smile and knew Lucy was right. She'd been at the receiving end of that smile. It'd said, *I know you're out of your league.* It said,

I dare you to do this. It said, *I can kiss you blind and make you like it.*

And her silly knees had weakened.

"If you need anything, anything at all," Lucy said. "Go to him."

If she needed anything, it was to really live for once. And though he both fascinated and terrified her, she thought maybe Chance could help. All she had to do was convince him of that.

"There's nothing he can't do once he sets his mind to it," Lucy said.

Yes, Chance was a man ready for anything, and if "anything" didn't come to him, he'd go looking for it. In that, really, he was the perfect one to help her out. "I'll be fine. You just get better."

"I'll do that." Lucy's eyes closed and she sighed deeply. "You don't mind if I take a nap now, do you, dear?"

"No, not at all." But Ally's stomach tightened, because if this visit was over it meant only one thing— she'd have to go out there and face Chance, the rebel with a cause who just happened to set her on fire. Not that she wasn't ready for this. She was. She just needed a few moments, that's all. "You rest. I'll wait here in this chair—"

"Oh no!" Lucy straightened, her light green eyes popping wide open again. "You mustn't wait. You just go on to the resort. And I don't want you to visit me often, it's too far. Come only when you can get away."

Ally hovered. "Are you certain?"

"Very." Again, Lucy laid back and closed her eyes. "I trust you as much as I need you. And Ally?"

"Yes?" Eagerly, she turned back, thinking there would be some miraculous reprieve.

"Give Chance a hug for me, would you?"

LUCY HAD THE GOOD sense to wait until the door shut completely behind Ally before bursting into laughter.

When the nurse came in a few minutes later, she was still grinning like a Cheshire cat.

"What's so funny?" the nurse asked, smiling a bit, because as Lucy knew, they all loved her.

She sighed dreamily. "Everything is just so perfect."

"You're in traction for the foreseeable future and everything's perfect?"

"I'm not going to die, am I?"

The nurse let out a startled laugh. "No, of course not. You're going to be fine."

Lucy stared at the closed door through which Ally had reluctantly disappeared. A knowing smile curved her lips. "Then, as I said, everything is perfect, just perfect."

CHANCE DROVE AS HE appeared to do everything else, with relish. His big hands mastered the wheel, his long, long legs flexed with muscle whenever he shifted. His intense gaze took in the sights as well as the road.

Ally was dying to approach him with her idea that he be the one to help her succeed at her little dream of being a wild adventuress. But though she felt him looking at her occasionally, he was silent.

Maybe half an hour into the drive, his cell phone rang. It was on the dash in front of her, and his wrist brushed her thigh when he reached for it. Her entire body tightened, but he didn't even look at her. He was looking at the caller ID with a frown.

"What's the matter?" she asked in an annoyingly breathless voice. *Get a grip*, she told herself.

"It's Lucy." He didn't even look at Ally, just brought the phone to his ear. "Couldn't even wait until we got there, huh?" he said into the receiver. "Curiosity was killing you, I suppose." His frown deepened. "I said I would, didn't I?... Yes, you mentioned that about her already. Three times, thanks. I get it. She's inexperienced and needs help." He looked at Ally, who wished with all her might she could disappear into a large hole.

"Look, it's done." He shoved a hand through his hair, which caused it to stick straight up. Instead of looking ridiculous, he looked...frustrated. Brooding. *Hot*. "I said I'd do it, I'd take care of her."

Looking away, Ally swallowed hard.

And listened unabashedly.

"Yeah, yeah, miss you, too," he said. "Now hang up, would you? And lose my phone number."

Ally whirled back, prepared to blister him about treating Lucy that way, when she saw that his mouth had curved in a fond smile.

The smile faded, however, the moment he looked at her. "We're almost to the resort." His voice was again rough with irritation, as if just the sight of her annoyed him. "I have work. You can go to Lucy's office or I can show you to the cabin that'll be yours for the duration."

He wanted to get rid of her. Preferably yesterday.

Too bad. "What are you going to do?"

"Be busy."

Without her, she got that. *Now*, she thought. *Ask him now. Tell him you need his help.*

But then they were driving up to the resort, and for a moment she actually forgot all about the unforgettable Chance. Leaning forward, she took in the huge three-story cabin that made up the main lodge, and the backdrop of glorious majestic mountain peaks behind it. It was breathtaking. Thrilling. And everything inside her tightened with anticipation. "Oh, it's gorgeous. I can't wait to explore."

"No. Don't go off by yourself." This was a demand as he got out of his big, bad, black Jeep that so suited him and slammed the door. Lifting a finger, he pointed it at her. "Don't wander. Don't even think about it."

She shut her door and let out a little, disbelieving laugh. "I thought my position here was higher than yours."

He leaned his butt against the Jeep and crossed his arms, treating her to a steady, unfathomable gaze. He suddenly seemed even taller than she'd thought, bigger and not at all friendly. "So?" he asked.

She decided to forgive him for being a jerk because

she needed him. Not that she'd ever admit that to his face. "So I'll do as I please, thank you very much."

"You're tired from your trip."

"Nope," she disagreed brightly. "And I don't need to rest. I'd like to get started."

"Uh-huh. And has it occurred to you that you don't know what you're doing?"

"You could show me."

He stared at her, then laughed. "No."

"Why not?"

"Because I'm too busy to baby-sit, remember?"

"Fine. I'll do it on my own." And she walked toward the lodge.

Chance watched her go, his mood darkening by the second.

Well, wasn't this just a picnic? Her curvy little body was practically quivering with imagined thrill. It was adrenaline and he, better than anyone, knew that.

So why was it both maddening *and* arousing to watch her?

Granted, he'd always been attracted to a woman willing to walk on the wild side, but he didn't want *this* woman to go wild on him. He wanted her gone before something happened to her, and something *would* happen. With her eager clumsiness and lack of experience, it was only a matter of time, and damn her, she'd do it on *his* watch, leaving him to deal with the aftermath of guilt and blame.

He had no intention of ever going through something like that again. Not even for Lucy, to whom he owed everything.

"Tell me things," she said, when she realized he'd followed her. She stood on the bottom step of the lodge and clasped her hands, looking so damn happy it almost hurt to look at her. "Tell me about this place."

"I have to meet a crew up on the mountain to work on the fire-damaged acreage."

"Please?"

He sighed, and had no idea why he obliged her. Pointing to the ski runs, devoid of all but a few patches of snow, he said, "We had an early spring this year. Skiing is over. To add to the fire reconstruction, we start work next week building two new quad chairs."

"I would have loved to try skiing," she said wistfully.

Chance could only be grateful for small favors. "If we hadn't caught one straight month of temps in the high fifties and sixties, we'd still be skiing. Or snowboarding."

"Do you even know how to snowboard?"

Both of them turned toward the voice. Though the boy who spoke wore the expression of someone grown and going on thirty; he was actually somewhere around fourteen. He slouched against the wall, scowling. The kid was Lucy's latest charity case, and a boy determined to drive Chance mad with his bad attitude.

Honestly, Chance had no idea why everyone couldn't just leave him the hell alone, but it never happened. For some reason, Brian always sought him out, and now Lucy had shoved Ally at him as well. "This is Brian Hall," he said to Ally. "He...works here. Ally is related to Lucy," Chance told the kid meaningfully. "She's taking her place for now. That makes her your boss."

"And yours," Brian pointed out.

Chance gritted his teeth. "Yeah."

"What is it you do?" Ally asked Brian, her smile warm and genuine in a way Chance hadn't yet seen from her. It so transformed her from simply average to beautiful, he found himself staring at her stupidly.

Brian just lifted a shoulder. "Stuff."

"Ah. I see." Ally looked amused, and again, Chance was struck by the change in her, by the genuine warmth and affection she showed Brian. Just looking at her, his chest went all tight, which he firmly attributed to hunger pangs.

"What kind of stuff exactly?" she asked Brian.

The kid kicked at the dirt in front of him. "I robbed a stupid store, got caught, got roughed up in juvie hall and then when they let me go, they said I started the fire here, so now I have to do even more stupid community service cleaning up the mountain."

Ally's smile faded. "You were roughed up?"

Now *both* Chance and Brian gaped at her. Was that all she'd heard? That he'd been roughed up? What about the stealing part? What about the fire part? Or the attitude screaming from him that said not only did he not care, but he intended to keep getting in trouble as long as it suited him?

"Were you hurt?" she asked, and got the famed

Brian shrug. He didn't know, didn't care, didn't remember. Pick any of the above.

"Brian?" Her voice was gentle but firm, and she dipped her head a little to be able to see his face.

"Not that bad," he admitted. A lie. He'd been beaten to within an inch of his life.

"It must have been awful." She spoke with such sincerity that even Brian dropped half his sullenness. "I hope you never have to repeat such a horrifying experience."

Brian did a good imitation of someone who couldn't hear, but Ally's smile was persistently sweet, and she made sure Brian saw it. "So...do you like being here?"

Brian shrugged again, though with far less attitude now. He even, slightly...stopped scowling.

It was nothing short of amazing. Chance couldn't believe it, and he stared at the kid in surprise before saying, "The judge decided that making him work here might make him understand what damage he'd caused."

"I didn't start the stupid fire," Brian said, his entire body going rigid again. "I keep telling you that."

"And I keep telling you, save it for the judge."

"Well," Ally broke in with a bright sweetness. "I look forward to working with you."

Chance watched with some amusement as Brian started to shrug again and stopped. In fact, he didn't snarl or swear, as was his habit. So far, only Lucy had managed to garner that much respect from him.

Then Brian gave Chance the sneer he'd spared Ally. "Can you really snowboard?"

"Yeah." He refrained from adding that he'd been a pro. "How about you?"

"Are you kidding?" Brian slid his hands into his pockets and rocked back on his heels. "I could go on the circuit if I wanted."

"Uh-huh." Chance shook his head, unimpressed. "Hard to do that from jail."

"I won't be in jail."

Chance hoped to hell not, but he had his doubts. Brian had grown up neglected and abused. By the time he'd turned seven, he'd been on the wrong side of the law. He'd already been arrested twice. He was sorely lacking in a positive role model, or any sense of direction for his life. Chance could only hope the mountain pounded some into him.

"Well, I know *I* could use help," Ally said. "I know next to nothing about the great outdoors. Are you going to be available?"

Brian seemed fascinated by this. "You're going to be the boss and you don't know what you're doing?"

She smiled, and again, it was a stunner. Her eyes glowed, her face lit up, and Chance found himself purposely looking away because he didn't want any spark of attraction clouding his brain and getting in the way of his simmering resentment. No, he was going to hold on to that for all he was worth.

"That's why I'll need a really great staff," she said.

Brian shot an indecipherable glance at Chance, then stared at the ground. "I'm not staff. Not really."

"Maybe that could change."

Now she was looking at Chance, too, the both of

them waiting with some sort of expectancy that made him groan out loud. "Did you somehow miss the part about *why* he's here?"

"No." Her eyes were full of warmth and compassion. A save-the-world, bleeding heart.

Dammit. "He's too young," he said. "Too stubborn." Though Chance himself had once been both, and Lucy had taken a chance on him. "He doesn't listen."

Brian's eyes flashed. "I will."

"With or without the attitude?"

"Without," Brian said between his teeth.

"Then prove it. But it'll have to be another day. I have to go clear the trails if we're ever going to open. And you're going to help," he said pointing to Brian.

"Me, too," Ally said.

Couldn't she see he just wanted to be *alone?* "In *those?*" he asked her.

She bent her head and looked down at her open-toed, dainty leather sandals. She wore a silver heart ring on the second toe of her right foot, which for some reason, seemed overwhelmingly sexy.

"I have some tennis shoes in my suitcase," she said.

He imagined a pair of useless white canvas shoes. "Ah, hell. Go to Ted in the General Store. Tell him to boot you up before you kill yourself. You, too," he snapped at Brian, who was wearing some sort of ridiculous black vinyl boot. "And hurry it up, would you?"

"You have such a way with children," Ally said dryly when Brian had left.

"He's not a child. Probably never was."

"Funny, I'd have said the same thing about you." She stared at the mountain, shielding her eyes from the sun. She bit her lower lip.

It was irrational. And really dumb, but Chance suddenly wanted to nibble on that full lip himself. Instead, he turned and walked away.

"Hey!" she called. "Where are you going?"

"Up."

"Wait for me."

"No." But he made the mistake of stopping to glance at her.

She looked as if someone had taken away her lollipop. Sweet. Innocent. Hopeful. He groaned out loud.

"I'm tougher than I look."

"That's good," he said. "You're going to need it. But you're still not coming with me, Ally. I've got all I can handle with Mr. Tough Guy."

She looked surprised at his use of her name, which he'd studiously avoided until now. "Brian's probably had good reason to be tough," she said.

"Yes." He hadn't expected her to be so insightful, though she was looking at him curiously, as if she could read him as well as she could Brian.

What did she see when she looked at him like that anyway? Telling himself he didn't care, he took his radio off his belt and radioed for Jo, his assistant, to come get her.

Let someone else take baby-sitting duty. He was done.

"I bet the two of you are a lot alike," Ally said. "You and Brian."

"That's ridiculous." And insulting. "He's just a kid."

"He clearly idolizes you. Wants to do what you do. That's a big responsibility. And dangerous, I imagine, given your apparent lifestyle."

"I don't want him trying to be me."

"I can see that." She slipped off his jacket and handed it back to him, leaving her standing there in her defiance and thin blouse. Her nipples pressed against the fabric, and his body stood up and took notice, further aggravating his temper.

Though she barely came to his shoulders, she kept her chin raised defiantly, despite the goose bumps all over her now. "Take it."

Take it.

Take *her*.

He had no idea where that irrational thought came from, but there it was, plastered across his brain, the image of him doing just that, taking her, her mouth wet from his, her eyes glazed over as he gripped her hips and—

He shook his head to clear it and grabbed his jacket. Already it held her scent, a light flowery one that was a complete contradiction of sweet sexiness, and as it had when he'd first looked into her eyes at the airport, his chest tightened.

Damn you, Lucy, he thought. *What are you trying to do to me?*

4

ALLY EXPECTED JO, Chance's assistant, to be every bit
as overtly male as Chance.

But Jo turned out to be short for *Josephine,* and while
she wasn't a man, she *was* tough as nails. Barely five
feet tall, with bright red, curly hair that bounced with
every step, Jo moved like lightning and talked at the
speed of sound.

"We'll get you geared up, but first let me fill you
in," Jo said after their brief introduction from the now
vanished Chance, who'd ditched Ally at his first op-
portunity.

Ally grumbled to herself about being deserted, but
had to admit, the disgruntlement might have come
from witnessing the enthusiastic hug Jo had given
Chance, the one where she'd pressed herself against
him like a suction cup.

He hadn't seemed to mind in the least.

Ally told herself she didn't care, but she had no intention of staying behind while he went up the mountain. Nope, she was going, too.

Jo was still talking ninety miles an hour. "I've got
your calendar for the week, and all the phone messages that have to be returned." The rest of her words
were tossed over her shoulder as she headed toward

the lodge steps, leaving Ally no choice but to run to keep up, straining to hear her words.

Jo just kept talking, not even looking back as they ran up the steps into the huge open-beamed lodge. "There's a stack of stuff that needs a quick reading and your signature." She made a sharp right and went up more stairs. As she moved, she consulted a clipboard. "There's five potential staff members to interview, that land permit to check over, and the new trails to discuss before mapping. After that you can talk to the fire inspector about your upcoming meeting and..."

Ally missed the next words due to the fact they were on their third flight of stairs and she was barely keeping up. She stopped for a second, her hand to her chest, sucking air into her poor lungs, wondering how long it would take her to get used to the high altitude, when Jo called out from the landing above.

"Where are you?"

"Here," Ally huffed, rolling her eyes at the slight irritation in the other woman's voice. Apparently they were all superhuman athletes here in Wyoming. "Coming!"

When she got to the third floor, Jo was just disappearing into the second office down the hall. By the time Ally got there, still panting as if she'd run a marathon, Jo was sitting in a chair next to a large desk, furiously scribbling notes and still talking as if Ally had been right behind her all the time.

"Oh," Jo said, startled, looking up. "What was the holdup?"

Ally dropped into a chair and struggled to catch her breath. "You're kidding me."

Jo didn't crack a smile.

Perfect. Attila the Hun. "I don't seem to be in quite the same physical peak that you are." Though she would be, come hell or high water. She was going to do whatever it took to do this right.

"You're out of shape?" Jo looked over Ally's body with a trained eye, and Ally squirmed, knowing what she saw—too many soft curves instead of tight, toned muscle.

Could she help it she favored cholesterol over exercise?

"What is it that you do again?" Jo asked politely.

"I'm a librarian." *Was* a librarian, she reminded herself, with the familiar pang for the loss of the job she'd loved. For the loss of life as she'd known it.

No matter. She was now going with gusto. Soon as she could breathe again, that is.

"I meant what do you do for exercise?"

"Oh. Um..." How to admit that exercise had always been at the bottom of her priority list, right next to getting her annual flu shot?

"You don't do any of it, do you?" Jo seemed disgusted. "No running, no swimming, no biking, nothing. I think I knew the truth when you put your jacket on the ski rack instead of the coatrack."

"Dead giveaway, huh?" Ally winced. "Well you might as well know right up front, I don't know much about this outdoor stuff, but I'm a quick learner." She smiled in what she hoped was a nonworried manner. "I'll be fine."

Jo remained unconvinced. "Chance is swamped right now. We're understaffed and overworked, and he's picking up all the slack."

"That's why I'm here. I'm going to start helping right now. I'm going with him to work on the fire-damaged trails."

"He's not going to like being held by back a novice climber."

Climbing? Not just walking up a nice, tidy path but *climbing?* Oh boy. Adventure number one, here she came. "Lucy asked me to help. I don't intend to be a burden. I want to lighten the load, not make it worse."

"Uh-huh." Jo's tone implied she doubted Ally would be much help in easing *anyone's* burden. "With Lucy in the hospital, Chance hasn't had a moment to himself to even breathe, and trust me on this one, he likes his time alone."

Gee, Ally hadn't noticed. "Like I said, I plan to help."

"The work is not only time consuming, but dangerous. And he's got Brian to deal with, dogging his heels, trying to match his every move—"

"That sounds even more dangerous."

"No kidding. The kid is trouble."

Ally reminded herself that she was no longer trying to save the world, no matter how much her heart squeezed. And it wasn't just Brian it squeezed for, but Chance, too. He might be tough, and gorgeous, but there was something in his dark eyes that called to her.

She hoped to ignore that call. "Maybe with an extra person around to help watch out for Brian, things will be smoother."

"Hmmph."

Ally's automatic apology for being who and what she was sat right on the tip of her tongue, but she swallowed it. She would *not* be a mouse, never again. "I may not know what I'm doing, Jo, but I can assure you, I intend to learn."

Jo softened slightly. "Well at least you have the best mountain manager available. Chance'll cover you, whether he likes it or not. He won't let anything happen to anyone on his turf."

Was he really that good at his job, or was Jo's clear adoration something more? Ally told herself she didn't care, but she couldn't get that hug Jo had given Chance out of her head. What would it be like to be plastered against that amazing body of his? "Has he been here long?"

"Ten years. His exploits on this mountain are legendary."

"He must have started young."

"Lucy once told me he came here before he was twenty, and as green as can be." Jo smiled. "Hard to imagine Chance being green at anything."

"But even he had to start somewhere." Ally leaned forward earnestly, never more determined. "I can do this, Jo. I understand your reservations, but I'm going to make this work."

Maybe she'd failed at being a librarian. At being a girlfriend. At just about everything so far, but she wouldn't fail at this, whether they believed in her or not. "Just show me where to gear up. And I'll be ready to go."

IT TOOK LESS THAN five minutes in the lodge shop to realize every single staff member—the same who had looked at Ally with their polite, distant and disappointed smiles—absolutely revered one T. J. Chance.

They respected him, emulated him.

Loved him.

If she could accomplish a fraction of that in her time here, she'd be ecstatic. By the time she got outside, wearing her new boots, leggings and a T-shirt layered with a lightweight jacket, Chance was gone.

"He just left," she was told when she asked about him.

Not a surprise. Determined, she took off on the trail pointed out to her, running, hoping to catch him.

Which she did, literally, only a moment later, when she came around a blind turn and plowed right into the back of six feet two inches of bad attitude.

"Sorry," she said when he whipped around to glare at her. But she wasn't sorry, not really. If anything, she was feeling that funny weak-knee thing again. And all because her hands had slid over his warm, solidly muscled back. Her nose twitched for another sniff of his skin. "You didn't wait for me."

He just looked at her.

"But I found you anyway."

"Yippee." He rolled his shoulders, as if just her presence brought him tension. "Now you can go back."

"No."

He sighed as if in great suffering. "Then stay out of the way."

"But I'm going to help."

A frown pulled at the corners of his mouth, and in response, she sent him a sweet but determined smile.

"Grab a shovel," he growled, pointing to where there was a small clearing. There were tools lying in boxes. "On the other side of that is the first foot trail, which can't be cleared by machine. There's already a few guys there working, including Brian."

"Okay." But he was already moving away from her. So she purposely switched her attention from him to her surroundings. The flames had wrought destruction all around her, taking away lush, healthy mountain side, leaving a charred, blackened, silent mess. It made her feel a terrible sadness.

Grabbing a shovel, she started in silence, sobered by the sight and how much work was in front of all of them. She thought of Lucy, and how worried she was, and that worry became Ally's, because she'd promised to help. She intended to keep that promise.

But after two minutes of lifting the shovel, her shoulders already hurt. She distracted herself by watching Chance attack his area.

She couldn't help herself.

The way his arms worked, muscles straining, skin tanned and taut and damp, was distracting. Up and down, he wielded that shovel, clearing the trail with a single-minded determination, never hesitating. It was mesmerizing, the way he was in total command of himself and all around him. It fascinated her.

He fascinated her.

Then his broad shoulders straightened as if he'd drawn a deep breath. He paused, feet wide apart, his hair blowing about his shoulders, surveying the destroyed land before him. Burnt pines towered above, shading him, throwing him in shadow, but she had no trouble sensing his deep sorrow. Then he turned and looked right at her.

She didn't look away, she couldn't. They just stood there for a long, tense moment, connected in some strange way she didn't understand. Then someone called him, and with one last unreadable glance, he walked away. His T-shirt clung to his back, and was shoved into those battered jeans so worn in all the right places. He could have been a model right off the pages of a glossy men's magazine.

Then she realized he was leaving. "Where are you going?" she called out.

He didn't so much as slow down.

So she dropped her shovel and ran after him. "Chance?"

He kept walking, forcing her to run to keep up with him. "To check on the higher portion of this trail."

Higher portion...sounded interesting. Her sense of adventure soared, filled her with giddy joy. "Are we going to leap off any cliffs?" she asked hopefully.

Chance stopped, then turned around and sent her a baleful look.

"Because I saw this outdoor show on the Discovery Channel one time," she told him eagerly. "And they showed how to—"

"We're not hucking anyone off a cliff today." He started walking again. "*Especially* not you."

"But—"

He stopped short, and once again, she plowed into the back of him. Because it had felt so wonderful before, she made sure to touch his back with both hands.

It still felt wonderful.

He turned on her. "Look, I realize your cabin doesn't get cable. Maybe you can buy a book and read about adventures instead."

"I can handle this," she said to his retreating back, wiping sweat from her brow because it was darn hot. "I could—" She stopped talking because he whipped off his shirt, apparently as hot as she was, and stuffed a corner of it into his back pocket.

She nearly stopped breathing. She'd known he was leanly muscled, perfectly defined. Magnificent. But she hadn't been prepared for him half-naked. Her fingers actually itched to touch, and she wondered if she ran into him yet again, if he'd know what she was up to.

It had to be the altitude, she decided. All the fresh air was going directly to her head.

Thankfully, her cell phone rang, piercing the quiet and removing her attention from the sexiest, sleekest, most amazing male back she'd ever had the pleasure of running into. Knowing it was one of her sisters, she sighed. It was really time to cut the cord, but just as she grabbed the phone from her pocket to tell her sister that very thing, she lost reception and it went nice and silent.

Ally smiled in gratitude for tall trees and high mountains. With any luck, she wouldn't gain good reception for days.

They walked. Or rather, Chance walked and she ran to keep up with him. In a matter of minutes, she was ready to expire. Humiliating as it was, she needed to stop. "I'll catch up," she gasped, sinking to a rock.

Chance came back to stand in front of her, hands on his hips, frown firmly in place. "Already? We've gone a quarter of a mile."

This unexpected dent in her new lifestyle was embarrassing, but only a temporary roadblock. "I'll be fine in a sec," she said, chugging air.

He looked her over from head to toe, slowly, then back up again, and when his eyes changed, darkened, even *more* heat suffused her. Nervous, she rubbed her palms on her thighs, then winced at the already developing blisters from shoveling.

Chance reached out and grabbed her wrist, turning her hand over to inspect her palm. "You're blistered already?" Cupping the back of her hand, he bent his head over it. His fingers were warm and calloused, and he lightly brushed his thumb across her sensitive skin.

A tingle ran up her arm, down her breasts and

pooled between her thighs. She snagged her hand back. "I'm fine."

"You're in terrible shape."

"Gee, why don't you tell me what you really think?"

He simply started walking again, until he realized she wasn't following him for a change. "Hurry," he said over his shoulder, but she shook her head because if she had to walk another foot right that minute, she was going to dissolve into a whimpering mass.

Stopping again, he tipped his head up and studied the sky as if hoping for divine intervention.

"Go ahead," she said. "I'll catch up."

"No you won't. You'll end up giving some bear indigestion."

"Nah, I'm too tough." She smiled at him, but it might have been a bit shaky because that bear bit had gotten to her. She peered into the woods around her, but didn't see any signs of big, hungry bears. "I'll be fine right here."

He didn't even attempt to hide his relief. When he started off again, Ally gave herself a moment to recover. Then she followed, knowing if she could only go at her own pace, she'd be fine.

And she was. Until she realized sometime later she no longer had the trail beneath her feet and she had no idea in which way she'd come.

Okay, no problem. But she was surrounded by three-hundred-foot lodge pines in every direction, and every one of them looked the same.

If you get lost, hug a tree and blow your whistle.

Yes she'd learned that from some kids' magazine she'd read while waiting in the dentist's office, but it was better than panicking. So she leaned on the closest tree, wishing for a whistle and her quiet, cozy, warm, friendly library job.

The woods were very noisy. A pine needle floated down, hit her cheek and she nearly croaked. They didn't have scary woods in the city.

How had this happened?

She was lost and was going to be some bear's lunch. With a sigh, she rested her forehead on the tree and started to give in to self-pity. She even thought about crying, but suddenly her watch beeped at the top of the hour, giving her the brilliant idea of setting off the alarm on purpose.

Beep, beep, beep.

It was an annoying sound, but one she hoped would carry through the thick, dense woods. Just like a whistle.

Bees buzzed. Something chirped. Something else, alarmingly close, rustled.

Beep, beep, beep.

How long could a human go without eating, she wondered. Would she freeze to death in one night, or would it would take more?

Beep, beep, beep.

"You've *got* to be kidding me."

Ally sagged in relief while pretending she didn't have a care in the world. Or that Chance's low, husky voice wasn't *exactly* what she'd hoped to hear. "Oh, there you are," she said as casually as she could while gratitude made her weak. "Just checking your rescue skills."

He laughed. "Yeah, right. Admit it, city girl. You were lost."

"Was not." Ally consulted her watch. "And I'm proud to tell you, you found me in less than twenty minutes. If I *had* been lost, that is." She smiled. "Which I wasn't."

"Turn off that alarm, it's driving me crazy and scaring the wildlife. And you were *so* lost."

"Okay, I'll admit I never got to the top of this mountain. But how about you—"

"Don't even say it. You're going back. I'm taking you to your cabin."

"I told you I don't need to rest."

"Fine, you'll go to the office then—where you'll stay if I have to handcuff you myself—and I'm coming back up here. *Alone.*"

Where he'd probably do something thrilling and reckless without her. Darn it. She was going to have to break him in slowly, she supposed. "Do you really have handcuffs?"

He smiled slowly. "Yep."

Oh, my. She followed him back to the trail, thinking about that and getting much warmer than the sun warranted.

Chance walked ahead of her in silence, probably satisfied he'd gotten things—*her*—under control. She watched his nicely muscled rear end for a moment and thought, *next time I run into that body, I'm keeping my hands out and low.*

Chance continued to completely ignore her.

"I'm sure by tomorrow I'll be a much bigger help," she said brightly.

His shoulders stiffened, and he might have even sworn beneath his breath, but he just kept walking.

NIGHT FELL QUICKLY in Wyoming. In all Ally's life, she'd never seen such utter darkness. No wimpy twilight hour for this place. One minute it was still daylight and the next, utter blackness had blanketed everything.

Sleep wasn't an option, not yet. The phone conversation she'd just had with Lucy reverberated in her mind. *Don't forget to enjoy yourself. For once pocket your worries and live.*

Ally liked the sound of that.

Yielding a flashlight, she walked the path from her small cabin to the main lodge, which looked deserted in spite of several lights burning. That was okay, she wasn't looking for company. Driven by a strange restlessness, she continued past the lodge, toward the sound of rushing water, which turned out to be a stream gone wild with the snow melt-off. A sign told guests where to rent rafts, another directed them to a natural pool several hundred feet down the path where swimming was encouraged.

Curious now, Ally moved closer to the water, squinting in the moonlight. There was a small building off to her left, and from what she'd learned from the extensive map Jo had given her, it was a storage shed. Inside would be rafts, canoes, kayaks—all sorts of water equipment.

An undeniable thrill raced through her, even though she was so sore from shoveling she could hardly move her arms. She could see herself in all that white water, rushing at dizzying speeds, screaming with excitement as she—

"Don't even think about it." A tall shadow stepped in front of her. With a gasp, she leaped backwards and might have fallen right into the river if two big, warm hands hadn't reached out to steady her.

"Easy," Chance said. "I'd hate to have to stand here and watch you drown."

She blinked and stared at his wide chest. Her stomach flip-flopped as she slowly raised her gaze past his mouth to his dark blue eyes. "You'd watch me drown rather than jump in and rescue me?"

He turned his head and studied the icy, rushing water. "Yes."

She didn't doubt him for a minute. "That might be bad publicity."

"You weren't worried about that earlier, when as GM you got yourself good and lost while walking on our easiest trail."

"I told you, I wasn't lost."

"You're sticking to that story, huh?"

Maybe it was his silky voice, or how the breeze carried the scent of his skin and tossed his hair about his shoulders. That, or the way he still practically held her in an embrace, but in any case, she was off balance.

She could feel the heat of him, all that barely contained strength and energy, and it made her shiver.

At the motion, he skimmed his hands over her arms. "Still haven't got your high altitude legs yet, I guess." He shot her a slow, suggestive smile. "I know several ways to combat that."

She was certain he did. "I'm...fine." *Coward.*

She felt his warm breath on her cheek and closed her eyes, wondering exactly what he could do to combat her sudden odd dizziness, and if it would involve that incredibly sexy mouth of his.

"You'll let me know if you change your mind," he murmured, and though he dropped his hands from her, he was still far closer than normal conversation dictated.

It lent an intimacy to their nearness she didn't know what to do with. "I'm okay."

"Sure?"

She was quite certain whatever he had in mind would only confuse her all the more, especially since the last time she'd seen him he'd been grinding his teeth to nothing, furious that she'd cost him precious time.

She lifted her hands between them to...what? If she touched his chest—his *amazing* chest—things would seem all the more cozy.

And yet she had the oddest urge to do just that. "I'm sure." But then she tipped her head back so she could see into his...*laughing* eyes! Hot temper filled her. "You think teasing me with...with *sexual* favors is funny?" she sputtered.

"I was offering *aspirin*." He cocked his head and lifted a brow. "And I have to say, I'm shocked at what *you* were thinking."

Now she did use her hands on his chest, to shove him back, but he was built like a solid brick wall. He simply and calmly stepped back on his own. "You know, Prim, I think I was mistaken." He scratched his chin and grinned. "I thought your eyes were plain gray, but they've got a lot of fire to them."

As if he cared what color her eyes were, or what made them burn. He had Jo, a woman who, no doubt, did *not* get lost on a simple trail. "I see you made it back from your second trip up the mountain," she said through her teeth.

"Always."

"And Brian?"

His amusement vanished. "Do you think I'd leave him up there?"

"No," she said, more than a little surprised at his fierce reaction. "I didn't think that."

"What *do* you think?"

That his voice could seduce a nun. That his tall, broad frame blocking the moonlight seemed strong and warm, so much that she had a silly urge to lay her head down on his chest and ask him to assuage all her yearnings.

"Brian is fine," he said. "Though I'm not responsible for him."

No, neither was she, but that didn't stop her from thinking about him, and worrying. It was a bad habit, wanting to fix the world, and everyone in it. *Ex*-habit, she reminded herself. She was no longer in the business of fixing anything or anyone except her own life. "I think maybe I should go catch some sleep."

He slipped his hands into his pockets. "How long are you going to do this?"

"What?"

"Stay here and play at doing Lucy's job."

"As long as it takes. And I'm not playing, I want to do it right."

"That's not possible. You got lost today in your own shadow."

"You're not exactly tame, you know. Why do you object to my new sense of adventure so much?"

He was shocked at her question. "Because *I* know what I'm doing. You, on the other hand, you're a walking nightmare."

"I can do this," she insisted. When would people stop doubting her? Stabbing a finger to his chest, she said, "I came here to work, and that's what I'm going to do."

He grabbed her finger, and short of a tug-of-war, she couldn't get it back. So she tried to look like it was an everyday occurrence to be holding hands with a near stranger. A tall, gorgeous, enigmatic stranger, one who thought she was a piece of fluff, one she was feeling a completely unacceptable attraction for. "I can be of help, Chance," she said. "If you'd only let me."

"Tall order for a woman who doesn't know what she's doing."

"I know how to wing it, and I've got determination on my side."

"You mean stubbornness."

"I'm going to be a good GM. I'm going to show the staff how good attitude works, and I'm going to show Brian how to learn to belong."

"And what makes you an expert on juvenile delinquents?"

"What makes *you* an expert?" Bold question, considering she didn't even know this big, rugged man with the glittering eyes so intent on her, but something reckless made her want to push him.

"I'm not," he said grimly, dropping her hand. "And don't want to be."

The night had turned chilly. The evening sounds hadn't abated, neither had the wind. And yet Ally was mesmerized by Chance's gaze, so much so that she couldn't have turned and walked away if she'd wanted to. Hidden fire, hidden pain, she realized with a shock.

His gaze held both.

And so had Brian's.

She nearly fell off the wagon right then and there, nearly let herself forget her new resolve, nearly let her heart jump into the fray, but she got a grip.

She was done taking care of people. She was! And anyway, Chance was completely self-reliant. Capable. Confident.

But God help her, she was drawn to those very things. Of its own free will, her gaze landed on his mouth. And of its own free will, her mind wandered...wondered.

He shook his head. "Stop it."

"Stop what?"

"Stop looking at me like that." His voice was little more than a growl.

"Like...what?"

"Like you want to be kissed." Eyes glittering, he took a step forward, so that barely an inch separated them, and she had to tilt her head up to see his face. Now if she so much as took a breath, their bodies would touch, chest to chest, thigh to thigh, and everywhere in between.

She didn't breathe. "I don't. Want to be kissed, that is." *Much.* She cleared her throat. "And I wasn't thinking any such thing."

"Liar." He tilted his head. Their mouths lined up perfectly.

Not that she was noticing.

He held himself perfectly still. So did she. Every single part of her was at war.

Kiss me.

Don't kiss me.

Kiss me.

"You weren't wondering?" he murmured. "Wondering what it would be like?"

"No."

"Wondering if maybe you could not like me and still want to kiss me?"

"No!"

"What about that hug?"

"What hug?"

"The one Lucy asked you to give me." His eyes sparkled mischievously. "I've been waiting for it."

She remembered Lucy's request at the hospital. *Give Chance a hug for me.* Not likely, not even if a part of her really wanted to feel all that dark, edgy beauty against her. "You'll be waiting a darn long time! And anyway, you're with Jo—" She broke off when he choked, then laughed. It was a full-belly gut laugh. Directed *at* her. "Why is that so funny, I'd like to know? I'd never... *lust* after a man who belonged to another woman." Or at least admit to it.

That made him laugh harder, but he finally got control of himself and simply grinned at her. "I'm not with Jo."

She went into self-denial over the relief that washed through her.

"I'm not another woman's man. I'm not *anyone's* man." His grin spread. "And you're really blushing now, you should see it."

Yes, she could feel the heat of it on her skin. How gentlemanly of him to point it out.

"Was it having to lie about not wanting to kiss me?" he wondered. "Or having to use the word...*lust?*" He whispered the last word in a high falsetto, in a perfect imitation of herself.

"Stop it."

"Come on, where's that sense of adventure you're always threatening me with?" He lifted a mocking brow. "Just admit it. You wanted to kiss me."

"Did not." But she couldn't help but wonder what

Chance, a man who greatly treasured his solitude and freedom, would have done if she had admitted the truth.

That for a moment, just a short one, she indeed wanted to kiss him.

ON HER SECOND NIGHT in the wilds of Wyoming, Ally got another call from Lucy.

"Having fun?"

Ally tucked the phone in the crook of her shoulder so she could continue to stoke the small fire she'd finally managed to start in her fireplace. The cabin was tiny and cozy, but icy cold, so it was necessity that had driven her to this, rather than the aesthetic value. It'd taken nearly an hour, and every single paper towel in the kitchen to get it going, but Ally was determined to get warm.

She only hoped she didn't have to use the toilet paper stock as well. "Am I having fun?" She'd taken three showers to get the lingering smoke smell out of her hair from the trail. She had mosquito bites in places no one should have to itch and her arm muscles were so sore from today's work she practically cried every time she moved. She blew a strand of hair from her eyes and sat back on her heels. Then grinned. "Yeah."

"Really? Oh, honey, I'm so glad. Tell all."

Ally used the poker, satisfied to see the tiny flicker of flame maintain itself. "Well, the trails are looking good. And I got on a bike today and didn't break anything."

Lucy laughed. "That's a great start."

Somehow Ally had convinced a staff member to show her how to ride, and given that she'd hit a tree on her first run, she was really doing remarkably well.

Even if she could hardly walk.

"Be careful," Lucy warned. "Watch out for the pesky rocks."

"Yeah, well. I'll try." She doubted she'd get another shot at it. Chance had nearly blown a gasket when he found out, and now no one would even talk to her, much less show her a good time.

"Tell me more. Is everyone treating you right? I worry, because though I love every one of them, my staff can be...well, rather snobby when it comes to the resort, but I'm sure Chance'll take care of you."

Oh yes, good old Chance. He'd take care of her. Of *humiliating* her, that is.

"He has, right? Taken care of you?"

"Why are we talking about me?" Ally asked, tossing another piece of wood to the fire. "How are *you*?"

"Bah! I'm as good as it gets. Now don't work too hard, Ally. We'll open when we're ready."

"You keep saying that, but I thought work was the whole idea."

"Good heavens, no!" Lucy sounded appalled. "You're to have the time of your life, do you hear me?"

Ally couldn't help but smile at her vehemence. "I hear you."

"Maybe you'll have such a good time, you'll want to stay forever."

Ally's amusement at the both of them quickly vanished. Slowly, she set down the poker. "Forever?"

"You don't have to sound so shocked."

"But..." She didn't have forever. She was here because...

Darn it.

Being here had nothing to do with obligation or family loyalty. It had nothing to do with her old life. She no longer *had* an old life—well, except for the apartment that she still had to get back to in order to close up, thanks to Mrs. Snipps, landlady from hell.

No, she was here because she'd wanted to do something purely for herself. She'd wanted to live, *really* live.

Still, it was temporary. When Lucy was better, Ally would go back and figure out what exactly to do with the rest of her life.

Forever wasn't an option.

"Ally? Would it be so terrible?"

She sounded a little down, and a horrible thought occurred to Ally. "You're not sick or anything, right? It's just your hip and ankle—"

"No, I'm not secretly dying and trying to prepare you, if that's what you're asking. I'm going to live to a ripe old age. I'd just like to do that with some family around, that's all."

"But...why me? I know the family is small, but there's my sisters and my parents—"

"Your sisters would never enjoy it here, they're far too spoiled for this life, though I do have hopes that'll change one of these days."

"It already has," Ally said grimly, thinking about how she'd told them just that morning, *again*, that they needed to work more hours to help pay for their own tuition. "They're going to grow up, whether they like it or not."

"Glad to hear it. And as for your parents, delightful as they are, they're just not interested in Wyoming, and I can't blame them for that. Look, honey...all I'm asking is for you to think about it."

As if she'd be able to do anything else. But fun as this may be, Wyoming wasn't her home.

"Oh, and if you want to jump Chance's bones while you're at it, that's fine with me, too."

Ally pulled the phone from her ear and stared at it in shock. "Lucy!"

With a loud cackle, she disconnected and Ally was left staring at the receiver, Lucy's laughter still ringing in her ears, and the words "jump Chance's bones" echoing in her brain.

It embarrassed her to admit just how much she'd thought about doing exactly that.

5

THE NEXT MORNING WAS cool and drizzly. Despite the weather, Chance decided to go ahead with the chair evacuation training he'd planned.

It meant everyone was going to be cold and wet for the next few hours, but in his opinion, this was a good thing. If he could have, he'd have trained everyone in a full-blown blizzard in order to simulate the worst possible conditions, but he'd settle for what he could get.

The faux evacuation was routine, performed throughout the year, and because he expected everyone on his staff to have hands-on training, all staff members participated.

He'd long ago learned the key to his success as a manager. Make it fun. Make it an adventure. Never let on that what they were doing was work, and hard work at that.

So he grinned in spite of the rain running down his neck, and rubbed his hands together. "Who's up for a ten-mile run to warm up?"

Everyone groaned.

"Good, everyone then."

More groans, and he laughed. "See? Chair evacuation training is a piece of cake."

"We're going to get hit by lightning," Jo grumbled, stuffing her wild red hair beneath a beanie knit cap.

"Nah, you're too ornery for that."

"There's a ton of paperwork to be done."

He flicked the tassel on her silly cap. "It's barely raining, and there's no lightning in sight. Besides, you hate paperwork."

"Oh yeah."

They all gathered beneath the operating ski lift, staring up at it as the rain came down.

"I don't hate paperwork at the moment," Jo decided.

Chance nudged her forward. "Guess who's first?"

"And to think I told Ally what a charming boss you were."

"I *am* charming." Not that Ally would agree, which of course was how he wanted it.

He'd dreamed about her, which had really fried him. He'd dreamed about how she would have tasted if he'd given into temptation, if he'd hauled her in his arms beneath that moonlit night and kissed them both to hot oblivion. "Let's get cracking," he barked, furious at himself for letting her get to him.

"Ever thought about becoming an officer in the army?" Brian asked, huddled beneath the steel lift with the rest of the staff. "You'd be good at it."

"Yeah, right. Military." That's the life his older brothers had chosen, not him. He ran his own life, always. "And why are you here? I thought you already worked your hours for the week."

"I did."

The kid's light cotton clothing was inappropriate for this weather, and he was already soaked to the bone, dammit. "So if you already worked," Chance said as patiently as he could. "Why are you getting wet for no reason?"

Brian muttered something beneath his breath and lifted a negligent shoulder.

"Speak up, would you?"

"He said he wants to make ski patrol."

Ally stepped into the clearing. She was bundled from head to toe today, which amused him. She looked...amazing, which didn't amuse him. She wore sleek black leggings tucked into boots. Her parka was nipped in at the waist, and her hood completely covered her hair, and nearly her entire face, so that all he could see of her were her eyes. They matched the stormy sky. "Well, at least you've got your own jacket," he noted.

"I try not to make the same mistake twice in a row." She met his gaze evenly, which surprised him. So did the dare he found glowing there. "Brian wants to be a part of this."

He started shaking his head before she even finished her sentence. "He's too young for ski patrol."

"Yes, but the training would be good experience."

"Hey, I'm already experienced." Brian straightened with a show of bravado that completely belied the uncertainty in his eyes, and the definite expectation of being rejected.

Damn, but something twisted inside Chance at that. No kid should look like that, no matter how irritating he was. "You want in when you're old enough, then you're in. If you're not in any trouble."

"I won't be."

"Whatever you say, Slick. But you have to be able to pass the Emergency Medical Technician course and keep up on the slopes."

Brian had gone utterly still. "I can do that," he said very seriously.

Chance was sure he would, or die trying. Still, he had to admit, it was nice to see that *something* meant so much to the kid that he'd forgotten to scowl. Everyone needed something to be passionate about, and being busy as hell just might keep him out of jail. "Then I guess you can consider this pretraining. Do you ever dress right?"

Brian looked down at himself. "This is all I have."

Ah hell. Why him? "Run up to the office and grab one of my rain gear sets."

Ally shot him a look of bright hope and affection, and deepening his scowl, Chance turned away from her. They spent the next half hour setting up the mock exercise. All but two of them would get on the running lift, then the two left on the ground would put the evacuation into effect. They'd take turns with that role, removing everyone off the lift, until each of them had the procedure down.

Through the set up, Ally remained on site, standing there in the rain. Chance ignored her. He went through the different possible scenarios with the staff, then spent some time demonstrating what to do in each of those instances.

And still Ally stayed.

And still he ignored her.

They were all drenched by the time the majority of them got onto the lifts for the first "rescue," including his new, and temporary, boss. Water ran off her rain gear in little rivulets. Her eyes were wide and clear and bright. *Excited.* She smiled at him, her long, long lashes spiked with rain, and something deep inside him tightened. Ached.

It pissed him off. She was too damn...bright. Happy. Vulnerable. And it made him feel vulnerable, too. He hated that. "What are you still doing here?" he asked in his most intimidating, go-away voice.

She smiled sweetly. "Same thing you are."

"No."

"No?" She tipped her head as if she didn't understand the word.

"Look..." He put his hands on his hips and gave her his scariest go-away look to match the voice. "Do you even know how to ski?"

"Well...no." She sent him that little smile again.

He kept his gaze on hers so he wouldn't think about kissing that little smile right off of her mouth. "So there's little chance you'll ever actually be on ski patrol."

"I want to learn this."

He sighed and remembered the phone call he'd gotten from Lucy just the night before. *Are you making her have fun? She's not had enough of that, Chance.*

Obviously Lucy didn't know what a pain in the—

though Chance noticed she was careful not to look down. "Sorry," she said. "Obviously my sister doesn't have a clue as to a what a real emergency is."

Chance would have said he hadn't thought Ally did either, but clearly there was a whole hell of a lot more to Ally Wheeler than he'd first thought.

The truth was, he knew little about her, except apparently she supported her sisters, which meant on top of the biggest, most expressive eyes he'd ever seen, and on top of her misguided sense of adventure that was going to be the death of him yet, she also had a deep loyalty streak.

Damn if that wasn't one of his favorite qualities.

He realized Jo was looking at him look at Ally. She lifted a curious brow.

He turned away.

Jo came up behind him. "I can't believe what you're thinking," she whispered.

"I'm thinking about lunch."

She laughed. "Yeah, right. *Lunch.*"

TWO HOURS LATER, they were on their fifth and final "rescue."

Ally's teeth were chattering, though her feet were thankfully and firmly planted on the ground as she watched yet another mock evacuation. Again and again her gaze was drawn to Chance as he directed the crew. Everyone, including her, looked like drowned rats.

Not Chance.

Darn him, but he looked good. He wore rain gear

like the rest of them, but his hat didn't make him look silly. It only emphasized his piercing dark eyes. There was a lock of wet hair dangling over his forehead, and his earring glittered. The five o'clock shadow on his face looked rough, exciting, and she wondered what it would feel like rubbing against her skin.

Locked in the fantasy, she imagined him going back to his cabin and stripping off his wet things until he was naked. He'd look really good naked, she thought on a sigh.

Then he looked over his shoulder, right at her, as if he'd heard her thoughts. An annoying little tingle went through her and she looked away first. But two seconds later she was looking at him again. Like a moth to the killer flame, she moved closer. "Maybe we should give them a break," she said, nodding to the tired staff.

"Them? Or you?"

She lifted her chin, wondering why he always stirred so much emotion within her. "It's one thing to risk injury because of an emergency, but there's no emergency at the moment."

"Oh, I don't know..." He shot her an innocent look. "I had to buy a new summer wardrobe and—"

She turned her back on his wide grin. "You know what I meant."

"I know," he said, his mouth so close to her ear she shivered. His eyes darkened at that little involuntary gesture. "But if there ever comes a time when we have to evacuate an entire lift of terrified skiers or snowboarders, any employee under my command needs to know what they're doing—blindfolded—bad weather or not."

"*Your* command?" But when she turned to face him, he'd already moved away.

"Break," he called.

The staff scattered at his welcome decree, every last one of them, including Brian. Ally went to leave as well, grateful not to have to admit she needed a breather too, if only to escape his all too consuming presence.

"Where are *you* going?"

She looked over at Chance, then wished she hadn't. He'd moved close again. He didn't seem bothered in the least by how wet he was. In fact, despite the water running off of his tall, muscled form, he seemed perfectly relaxed and in his element. A drop ran down his temple. Across his jaw. He'd removed his hat, and when he looked at her, when their gazes were locked, he sucked a raindrop off his lower lip.

Heat suffused her. Her skin felt too tight. Her tummy fluttered. It was irrational, it was stupid, but she wanted to run a finger over that wet jaw, wanted to lean close and lick a drop off his skin herself. She wanted to touch him, taste him. "You...called for break. Everyone left."

"Yes, because everyone else knows how to get off a lift."

"I just got off one."

"No. You were evacuated. As in physically removed."

"Oh." She eyed the lift. It looked so easy now that

the thing was stopped. "Well, how difficult could it be?"

He laughed at her of course, he always laughed at her. He walked over to the control booth and turned the lift back on. The chairs started to move. Unclipping his radio from his belt, he brought it up to his mouth and told Jo they'd be right back, that he wanted Tim on radio for back up.

"Get on," he said to Ally, gesturing with the radio still in his hand. "This is a beginner run, we can walk back down from the top."

"We?"

"Yeah." His body brushed hers when he walked past her. "*We.*"

Her stomach tightened again, and not from fear this time.

THEY GOT ON TOGETHER, though Ally did her best not to touch him. Chance did his best to make sure she had to, so that by the time they were settled, they were shoulder to shoulder, hip to hip and thigh to thigh. Everywhere they touched, he burned for more, and it really got his temper going. "Tired?" he asked, wanting to hear that she was, that she couldn't wait to hightail it home any second.

Nice guy that he was, he'd drive her back to the airport.

"Of course not." Her knuckles were white from the grip she had on the steel chair. Her pupils were huge. She was clearly doing everything in her power to pretend she wasn't high above the ground. Moving. "I thought you were a wild, risk-taker kind of guy," she said, looking resolutely ahead. "Why would you call Tim for backup when you can handle anything?"

"Because getting on a lift without anyone knowing would be stupid, especially if something went wrong."

She swallowed hard. "Wrong?"

"Yeah." He looked at her profile. So proud. So pretty. So petrified. "For instance, you could freak out on me."

"I'm trying to keep my freaking to a minimum, thanks." She continued to cling to the side of the chair, and he realized that some sick part of him wanted her to cling to *him*.

"I talked to Lucy this morning," Ally said shakily, then glanced at him. "She said she knew how much she was putting on you, and that she was very grateful."

Well, damn. Add guilt to his current list of sins. Topping that list was lusting after city girl here.

The lift jerked and Ally quickly closed her eyes. "She said you've always been there for her."

"And vice versa."

She opened one eye, and when the lift remained smooth, then the other. "How did you get started here?"

"I was tired of wandering from place to place. Lucy hired me for ski patrol."

"You were...just wandering the globe?"

"Yep."

"You don't have family?"

Damn, now she pitied him, the last emotion he required in a woman. "My parents traveled a lot back then. I ended up in Wyoming looking for trouble." Tina had just died and he'd spent some lost months drinking and risking his life away. Lucy had given him what he'd never known he was missing, what he never would have allowed anyone to give him if he *had* known—stability.

He'd soaked it up.

Within two years he'd been running the ski patrol. Two more and he'd been in charge of the entire resort, second only to Lucy as general manger. In his opinion, he had the best job in the world, with a nice chunk of downtime every autumn, which he used to roam far and wide, just to get it out of his system.

Africa, South America, India, everywhere and anywhere he chose.

But he always came back, *always*.

The lift dipped a little, and Ally drew a shaky breath. "You were good with Brian today," she said quickly. "Even though you're not exactly a compassionate, sensitive caretaker."

"I'm not his caretaker. He just works here."

"I suppose he paid for those new boots he's wearing, the ones that have Sierra Peak Resort plastered on the sides?"

Chance watched her grip the chair with her fists when it jerked again. He watched her bite her lip, watched her breasts jiggle, her thighs press close together. He stared into her big, gray eyes and felt his body tighten. Specifically, his lower body. "So he needed new boots."

"So you care in spite of—" She broke off when he put one arm along the back of the chair, the other across the front of her on her arm grip, effectively trapping her within his embrace. If he'd thought her eyes big before, they nearly popped out of her head now. *"What are you doing?"*

"In spite of what?" he inquired softly.

"In spite of the fact—" She looked down at the ground, then paled again. "That I should just keep my thoughts to myself."

"Oh no, you don't." He brought her chin around, which meant he had to touch her. Big mistake, but that didn't stop him. Her skin was as smooth as silk.

She licked her lips, and gave away her inner most thoughts by darting a quick glance at his mouth before lifting her gaze to his. "I was just going to say...there's a lot of similarities between Brian and yourself. It's in the eyes."

"Really." Now *he* couldn't stop looking at *her* mouth. White skin. Pink mouth. White and pink. He imagined she had white thighs and pink nipples, and nearly groaned. "And what would that similarity be?"

"Well..." She laughed a little. "You're probably not going to like it."

His eyes narrowed as he tried to keep track of the conversation while picturing her naked. Not an easy feat. "Try me."

"I see a...dark neediness," she whispered. "In both of you. An emptiness." Her voice softened, so did her eyes. "You need someone to care about you, Chance, to look after you. And much as I wish otherwise, I promised myself I wouldn't do that anymore."

"You..." She'd actually done it, rendered him speechless. "You think I need taking care of?"

"Yes."

Shock turned to genuine amusement, and he laughed so hard he nearly fell off the chair. "Look, Prim, I've been taking care of myself since I could talk. I don't need anyone, I never have." He sobered and thought of Tina. "Never will. Thanks for the laugh though, especially considering *you're* the one who needs a keeper."

She sputtered over that for a moment, until the lift jarred again, hard. It happened twice more, jerking them both, and scaring a gasp out of Ally. When it hiccuped for the forth time, she let out a sound of pure terror and threw herself at him, doing as he'd wished for only a moment before, clawing her way right into his lap.

He put his arms around her curvy body. If he hadn't, she might have fallen out of the chair, but that's not what he was thinking of as his hands slid up her slim spine. She fit against him as if she'd been made just for him. Her legs were entwined around his. Her rib cage felt small and fragile beneath his hands, but her heart was pounding powerfully enough. "Yeah," he murmured. "*I'm* the needy one." He'd meant to say it teasingly, but the feel of her, the warm, soft, womanly feel of her, overrode all brain activity, and his voice came out low, husky. Rough. He found his arms tightening around her, his mouth unbearably close to hers, and their gazes locked.

She whispered his name. It was an invitation, one he almost took. After all, he truly loved women, all of them, and even though *this* woman was particularly irritating, and most definitely in his way, there was something about her. Not to mention she just happened to be in his arms, pliant and willing. But he wasn't so far gone as to forget the problems that came along with her. First, she was going to drive him to the loony bin. Second, city girl or not, he seriously doubted she was made for the hot, passionate—and short—kind of relationship *he* was made for. No, despite the fact she thought she wanted wild, she really wanted the guy who had an office job, a regular nine-to-fiver, a man who'd give her a nice home, a minivan and at least two kids.

That was so far from his own life he shuddered.

But damn, she felt good. He closed his eyes and tried to recite the reasons this was a bad idea.

"Chance?"

Actually, if he was being honest—and he always was, at least with himself—he could really get used to the way she said his name, especially if she was naked and spread out for him in his bed...now *there* was an image, one that would stay with him for the rest of the day.

"Chance!"

Oh yeah...the way she said it made him hard as rock. "Hmm?"

"We're at the top." And while he was still stupid with the lusty images she'd planted in his head, she leaped down with surprising grace and walked away.

6

THE RESORT WAS HOPPING, even though it was off-season, and Ally was truly, overwhelmingly busy. She couldn't believe the amount of paperwork it took to run the place. Or the phone calls. Not to mention the nonstop coming and going of various staff members, the planned activities and even the volume of food consumed on a daily basis.

The sheer size of it fascinated her. The immediate land around the cabins and lodges were owned by Lucy. But beyond that—the ski runs and trails, all the way to the summit, was leased.

And burned.

On Ally's second week, the trails were finally useable. They'd spent hours and hours reseeding and planting, helping Mother Nature along. They were finally ready to open for summer season. When Chance made the announcement, everyone cheered, then celebrated with pizza. Ally drove a resort Jeep to the hospital, and Lucy got so excited she nearly fell out of her hospital bed. Then she sent Ally back to celebrate with everyone else.

With Lucy out of commission, it was Ally's job to deal with most of the paperwork, which included insurance. Thanks to the fire, their insurance company wanted to triple their premiums. Ally wasn't a degreed accountant, but it didn't take one to realize the truth—the cost was exorbitant.

When she tried to talk to Chance about it, he shook his head. "We'll earn it back, don't worry."

"Don't worry," she repeated, never more reminded of their basic differences. While he was the wild rebel, she was only a wanna-be. "This isn't small change we're talking about. And it's *annual.* Thanks to the fire, Lucy will have to pay this much *every* year."

"You're not looking at the big picture." He'd just come in from outside, where the weather had turned unseasonably hot and windy. His hair was tousled, his face tanned, and if he'd shaved, it'd been several days. He wore a loose-fitting black tank top and hiking shorts that showed off beautifully sculptured legs. The clothes weren't designer, they weren't even close to new, but she couldn't take her eyes off him.

Never before had she figured appearance an important part of a person, but she'd certainly never felt her mouth go dry and her tongue twist itself in knots over a man's attire either. Not like now.

He was truly drop-dead gorgeous.

He caught her looking at him, or specifically at his shorts, and the most interesting way they outlined his every nuance and muscle. Clearly enjoying himself, he leaned backed against her desk and crossed his booted ankles in a casual pose. "Do I have toilet paper on my shoe?"

"Um...no."

"Are my clothes on backwards?"

He wore the unconcerned expression of a man deeply confident enough not to care if he *was* sporting toilet paper. "No."

"See? I told you I could take care of myself." Then he grinned, and since for once he wasn't laughing at her, the smile was totally disarming.

Trying not to give in and laugh, which is what she suddenly wanted to do, she stared at the paperwork spread out in front of her and saw none of it.

What was it about him that made her want to both smack and kiss him at the same time? She'd never had this problem before. Always she'd been able to withdraw into herself, even with Thomas, *especially* with Thomas. But somehow, some way, Chance drew her. "The big picture," she repeated with effort. "Tell me."

"This resort has made a name for itself because of our trails. We've just redone them, and added new ones. We're acquiring more land from the land trust. We're constructing new lift operations. And because of all that, I can lure athletes from all over the world."

His sureness staggered her. Not because it was false, but because she was beginning to realize he could back up everything he said. For all purposes, it *was* his mountain, his trails, his reputation that made the place.

She wanted a fraction of that belief in her own abilities.

"Now I can do even more," he told her. "Because of the new trails we opened, we can offer certain events, *televised* events, that will bring recognition. And more revenue."

It was exciting, thrilling, and she felt her sense of adventure soar. She imagined herself involved, handling television crews and famous celebrities. "What can I do?"

"Absolutely nothing."

"I'm general manager, remember?"

"You're a walking catastrophe, is what you are."

"I won't get hurt."

"I can bank on that since you'll be right here in the office—"

"While you have all the fun? No way."

He looked her over, starting at the hiking boots she was so proud of because they no longer gave her blisters, working his way upward past her walking shorts, past her blouse, though he lingered there long enough to have her nipples pressing against the material in response.

It was crazy, that just a look from him could do that to her.

A lazy, knowing smile curved his lips. "Are you looking for fun, Ally?"

His voice was soft, seductive, and his eyes half-closed and sleepy. Sex appeal oozed from his every pore and her body reacted. "On the mountain," she said through her clenched jaw. "I'm looking for fun on the mountain."

"You can't handle the mountain."

"Oh, for Pete's sake! You act like you've never done anything reckless in your life! I've seen pictures of you skiing, you know."

His eyes glittered at that, and pushing away from

her desk, he moved toward her, leaving her wavering between holding her ground and running. "You've never seen me in action," he said softly.

No, she hadn't, but she could imagine just how good his tall, rangy and oh-so-fit frame would look on the slopes, his long legs tearing up the snow as he worked his way effortlessly over the roughest terrain. "This isn't about *you*," she managed.

He stopped close enough to touch, but he didn't. She looked up into his eyes. A mistake. They were dark, deep and full of heat. Oh man, he was something all charged up.

"No go."

"No go?" she repeated, needing to press, needing to stir her anger so that she could keep her mind on track, instead of wanting to investigate such things as what his mouth might feel like on hers. "Why are you always so quick to dismiss me?"

He placed a finger against her lips. "This isn't about the mountain."

"It's not?"

"It's about you. And me. Don't lie," he said when she opened her mouth to do just that.

His gaze was intense. *Sexual.* And her breathing changed.

So did his. "No more games," he whispered.

Undoubtedly, she could have ducked beneath his arm and lengthened the space between them. He wasn't holding her, he wasn't even touching her, though she could "feel" every single hot, powerful inch of him.

The silence stretched out. Neither of them moved, neither spoke, though Ally's insides were screaming. He was so close, so warm, so big. The tension tightened within her, and it wasn't an unpleasant tension, but something different, something undeniable.

"I've warned you about looking at me like that," he said in a low voice.

"I know." But she kept doing it.

"I won't be your latest adventure, Ally."

"Why not?"

He let out a rough laugh. "We're too different."

"That I noticed." He wasn't attracted to her. It was a sobering fact. She'd always wanted to feel the sexuality most women seemed to feel, and make a man feel it in return, but she hadn't, not with Thomas, not with anyone. "I understand." It wasn't as if she'd had expectations—okay, maybe she had. But who wouldn't? He was so beautiful, so uninhibited, so damn hot. "I don't do it for you."

"You don't what?"

She looked up into his eyes. "You know, make you horny."

"No?" Snagging her hips in his hands, he rocked them to his, *hard*, so that she couldn't help but feel the long, heated bulge behind his zipper.

"Oh," she whispered.

Their bodies brushed together again and every bit as affected by their nearness as she, he drew in a harsh breath.

Encouraged, she lifted a hand to stroke his jaw, because she'd been dying to do that all day.

Only he caught her fingers in his and stopped her. "Don't."

The word seemed torn from him. "Kiss me," she whispered.

He stared at her. "This is a really bad idea, but for the life of me, I can't remember why."

"Good."

"Remind me."

"No way." Then because he was holding her hand, and her other was wrapped around his neck, she tugged until she could slide her cheek along his. "Kiss me, Chance, come on, just one kiss."

Another rough laugh rumbled in his chest, and he slid his fingers into her hair, lifting her face, looking into her gaze for a long moment before lowering his mouth to just the corner of hers. He dabbled there, then nibbled his way to the other corner, making a deep sound of pleasure at the taste of her. "Tell me no."

"Yes."

"*Ally.*"

Her insides melted at the sound of her name on his lips, then dissolved completely when he tilted her head to match up their mouths.

It should have been just one simple little kiss. Only there was nothing simple or little about it. Her senses revved, her legs weakened. Her heart soared, and she murmured his name, wanting more, so much more.

He complied, drawing one hand down her spine to her bottom, squeezing, pressing her even closer. His other cupped the bare skin of her neck, his thumb stroking her jaw as his mouth teased and coaxed hers.

When he pulled back, she gripped his shirt in her fists and held on because the connection had become far more important than breathing.

"You said one kiss," he reminded her, his eyes dark, his voice raspy and rough.

"I lied."

A low moan escaped him, then he kissed her again, long and slow, wet and deep, taking his sweet time. This time when the kiss ended, they were both panting, and he rested his forehead against her brow. "You're not what I planned on."

"What did you plan on?"

"Not feeling as though you've blown into my life like a fist to the gut, that's for damn sure." His mouth was still wet from hers, and he looked hot and bothered.

That made two of them.

Only his brow was furrowed with intensity, his eyes filled with mysteries and secrets he had no intentions of sharing with her. And looking deep into his gaze, she knew the truth. She was going to be leaving here all too soon, and she'd done what she'd sworn not to do.

She'd gotten her poor heart involved.

TWO DAYS LATER Chance found himself filling in on mountain bike patrol. It was hard, hot work, and though he'd never had a problem with that, by the end of the afternoon, after warning oblivious first-timers of the danger of leaving the trail, after chasing not so oblivious bikers who should have known better against the same thing, he longed to rip down the steep terrain, tearing up the dirt, wind flying in his face.

Longed to break all his own rules.

How he'd ended up with so many rules to begin with was beyond him. When he'd left home at age seventeen, his parents had welcomed his restlessness with pride, sending him off with smiles as he'd backpacked across the globe, getting into one scrape after another and loving every moment of it.

Until Tina.

After her death, he'd somehow landed in Wyoming, with twenty bucks and a tired spirit. The remoteness, the sheer vastness, the very wildness of the land called to him as nowhere else ever had.

Luckily for him, Lucy had taken one look, and had hired him on the spot. He'd been given a tremendous amount of freedom, coupled with all the thrill and adventure he could make for himself.

And he'd made plenty. He needed some now.

The minute the mountain closed to paying customers, the second he ripped off the vest that qualified him as an authority figure, he put his bike over his shoulder onto his back and climbed the mountain so he could go down his way—mind-blowingly fast. No responsibility. No Brian dogging him. No Ally blinking her big eyes at him.

Nothing but his own company.

Halfway up, the radio on his hip crackled. Damn, he should have turned it off.

"Hey, boss," came Jo's voice. "Lucy on line two. She wants to tell you not to break a leg."

Chance smiled and kept going, his muscles straining, his breath coming in even pants, breaking a sweat for the first time all day.

"She also wants to know if you've been kissing Ally."

He stopped short, nearly tripped over his own two feet.

"Don't worry," Jo said, laughing at his silence over the airwaves. "I told her City Girl wasn't exactly your type."

Which was absolutely true. He didn't want her, certainly didn't need her, no matter what she seemed to think. Just the idea she considered him needy at all really got to him.

She was the needy one, dammit.

He hiked on, refusing to waste precious biking time thinking about it, or her. Or the kiss he could still feel on his mouth even now.

But one hundred yards later, he stopped at the unmistakable signs that he was being followed. Soon enough, Brian appeared, wearing a defiant look and carrying a bike that had seen better days.

Chance swore. "What are *you* doing?"

Brian's chin went up a notch. "Same thing as you."

"You're checking out the terrain, making sure all the guests are down the mountain?"

Brian snorted. "That's not what you're doing.

You're climbing up so you can rip down, fast as you want."

Chance stared at him, then sighed. "Okay, fine. You caught me. Now go away."

"I want to come with you. I want to learn all I need to know about this place."

"Well, that sounds suspiciously responsible."

"I'm not stupid."

"And yet you're a juvenile delinquent. Go figure."

Brian's face reddened. "I didn't start the fire."

"Yeah, yeah."

"I didn't!"

Chance no longer knew what he thought on that score. Brian seemed genuinely indignant about the charge. On the one hand, if Brian *had* started the fire, he was being suitably punished. But if he hadn't, as he continuously claimed, then Chance had been pretty rough on him.

"Can I go with you, or what?"

Chance shoved his fingers through his hair, wondering why he couldn't just say no. He was going soft, no doubt. "Yeah. Fine. Whatever."

He hadn't realized the tension that had held Brian rigid, but the boy relaxed now, enough to let out one cocky grin. "Yes!" He ran up the trail toward him, half carrying his bike, half dragging it.

Chance watched, torn between the need to groan with frustration and the need to smile at the enthusiasm he recognized all too well.

Still, he'd rather be alone. He was a simple man with simple needs. He wanted to live his life the way he wanted, when he wanted—without restraint. Work wasn't considered a restraint, he loved his work. But Brian on the other hand, the kid was a definite restraint.

As was Ally, with a capital R.

And as if he'd played with fate at just the thought, he summited the mountain with Brian dogging his heels and came to an abrupt stop.

There at the top, pretty as a picture, smiling with hope and excitement, stood Ally, a mountain bike leaning against her hip.

"What in the hell are you doing here?"

"Inappropriate language," she tsked, picking up the helmet dangling from her handlebars and putting in on her head.

Backwards.

Swearing, then biting his tongue at the grin Brian gave him, he strode forward and pulled it off. His fingers slid through her silky hair as he turned the helmet around. The scent teased him and he scowled. "How did you get up that trail and why are you here, *here* where *I* am?"

"I walked up the trail," she said. "Same as you, soon as I heard you tell Jo on the radio what you were going to do." She smiled sweetly and something inside his chest did a slow roll. "I waited for you. As for why, it's because here is where you are."

How did he respond to that? With one look into her wide, guileless eyes, his usual sarcasm failed him. "You don't know how to ride. You hit things. You fall."

"I've been practicing. Every afternoon in the parking lot."

"The parking lot is flat."

"I'm doing this. *We're* doing this." She turned to Brian. "Now I want you to be extra careful, do you hear me?"

Brian was still grinning. "I hear you. Can I lead?"

"If that's okay with Chance," she said demurely.

Oh, *now* she was being meek. "Go ahead," he said tersely, wondering if he purposely lost both of them up here, if they'd make it down on their own.

He wouldn't bet on it.

So together the three of them came down the newly redone trails, the wind in their faces, trees whizzing by, the earth crunching beneath their wheels, and though everything inside Chance screamed to race down the trail at eye-popping speed, he restrained himself. *Barely.*

It helped that Ally's T-shirt was white and snug. It helped that the wind left her chilled, which meant her nipples were clearly defined. It helped that she had the best butt he'd seen in a good long time—

"Let's go off trail," Brian yelled.

It was exactly what Chance wanted, *needed,* to do, and he warred with himself, but in the end, he shook his head.

"Why not?" Ally asked.

Yeah, why not?

"It's against the rules," he said, wincing at his militant tone. He took the lead and stayed on trail. While pedaling, watching his world go by, he took a good hard look at himself and didn't like what he saw one bit.

How had *he* become the pansy and *Ally* the wild thing? He couldn't help but think about how she'd felt in his arms, lush and warm, eager and pliant, whimpering into his mouth for more. Passionate. Uninhibited. *Ready.* At that thought, his foot slipped, and the next thing he knew, he was face down in a heap, eating dirt.

"Wow." Brian leaped off his bike and ran toward him. "That was an awesome fall. You okay?" The kid looked over his shoulder, then leaned close. "Were you trying to show off?" he whispered. "You know, for Ally?"

"Oh, Chance!" From behind them came Ally, still riding, her legs pumping for all they were worth, her hair flying, her mouth opened in a little "Oh!" of concern. She came closer and braked—too late.

She was going to crash, hard, and all Chance could do was watch in horror as she skidded past him, screaming like a banshee.

A small bush broke her fall.

Surging to his feet, Chance rushed toward her, sinking to his knees at her side as visions of her dying choked him so that he couldn't even breathe. "Ally," he managed, only to have her get up on her own, laughing at herself as she dusted herself off. "I'm fine," she said, an innocent hand to her breast. "How about you?"

He sank to his butt, the adrenaline catching up with him. Then, because he was too weak for even that, he lay back on the ground, studying the sky, waiting for his heart rate to return to normal, which it probably wouldn't do until Ally left Wyoming.

"*Chance?* Are you okay?" She leaned close and peered curiously into his face. "How are you?"

How was he? Crazed.

Brian was trying to hold back his amusement at having watched his idol fly over the handlebars like an amateur, but he failed as a laugh escaped him.

Chance glared at him. "Oh yeah, this is just hysterical."

"You're not supposed to think about a chick when you're doing something dangerous."

"Gee, thanks for the tip." He looked at Ally, who was applying lip balm to the mouth he hadn't been able to stop thinking about for days.

"Can we go off trail now?" she asked, a branch in her hair, dirt on her cheek.

"No."

"But you do it all the time."

"I have terrain to check out."

Brian gave out that snort again.

Ally just looked at Chance, her huge eyes filled with disappointment, though why it mattered what she thought, he had no clue. By her own admission she didn't want to care about him, she had enough on her plate.

So did he.

Still, he made them all stay on trail, despite Brian's grumbling. He stayed on trail and watched Ally's nicely rounded bottom as it bounced in her seat. He'd never ridden with an erection before, and learned the hard way it was a definite detriment to his well being.

7

DETERMINED TO FIT IN, Ally exercised every night. She worked hard every day as well, doing all the paperwork in the office, helping on the mountain, replanting. And with Lucy's request in mind, she made sure to fit in lots of fun as well. Every lunch hour she spent learning something new.

This week it was kayaking.

It took a lot of convincing, but she got Tim to take the same lunch hour, which he spent showing her the basics.

One morning they got up early and hit the river for an hour before work. Afterwards, exhilarated, still wearing the neoprene river jacket Jo had lent her, and a pair of small men's swimming trunks, she stood on the path between the lodge and her cabin. She was wet, and she needed a hot shower, but it was a glorious morning. There were heavy woods on either side of her, so that if she looked up into the amazing sky she could almost believe she was all alone on earth.

Birds sang. Trees rustled. Branches crunched beneath her feet. All sounds that only weeks ago had made her so nervous. Now she thought them lovely. Essential. She hadn't heard them often enough in her city.

She had to laugh at that, because San Francisco had never been *her* city, but a place where she'd parked herself and let life pass her by.

She couldn't fathom doing that now. Over the past three weeks she'd felt more vibrant, more alive than she'd ever felt, even in her precious library. Yes, she missed take-out food. She missed a good shopping mall. But breathing in the fresh, clean air, Ally suddenly couldn't imagine the crowded freeways, the pollution.

A female giggle pierced the air and the woods went completely silent.

"Anyone there?" Ally called down the empty path, imagining a clandestine meeting between destined-but-tragic lovers. Maybe they had sneaked away into the forest, overcome by passion. Maybe they were fated to steal moments in time, trapped by circumstance, by a family feud, by social differences...

The only tragedy here was her imagination, though she couldn't deny the little sigh and the wish that *she* had a lover to meet. A lover like...oh darn it, she might as well admit it. Like Chance. Just the thought of him, all dark and brooding, heated and aroused, made her weak.

As if it could ever happen. Laughing at herself, she started walking again, but didn't get two feet before she heard another giggle, followed by a distinctly male "hush."

"Okay, I definitely heard that," she said to the trees.

More unnatural silence, though she could have sworn that "hush" had sounded like...*Brian?* But it was a weekday, which meant he'd be getting ready for school.

Or he'd better be.

Not that she was worrying about him. No, that would mean she wasn't following her new pattern for life—*Ally first*. But there was something about him, so tough yet so vulnerable, that if she *had* been the old Ally—and that was a big if—then she would have ached to help him.

As if he'd ever let anyone do that for him.

Hopefully he'd find his own way, and that it would be a safer, more grounded path than the person he so clearly idolized—T. J. Chance. Because while she was enjoying living the wild life during her time here, she knew it couldn't last, just as she knew it wasn't the lifestyle for a fourteen-year-old. Not with his fondness for adventure, his dislike for authority, and a definite penchant for danger. Even his girls weren't picked with care. Jo had told her Brian was "hanging" with one whose father was an owner of a competing resort, a man who'd undoubtedly look at Brian's baggy clothes and sullen expression and hate him on sight.

A twig snapped.

"Darn it!" She stopped again. *"Who's there?"*

More silence greeted her. No reason to feel this frustration. So there were two people having a grand old time in the woods, when she had a deep longing to have a grand old time in the woods herself. So what? It didn't mean she had to become irritable simply because the only man she wanted didn't *want* to want her back. She began walking again, faster, frustrated. "Damn him anyway."

"Talking to yourself again?"

She nearly fell over. That very man she'd been thinking about stood on the steps of the lodge as she came out of the woods. His big body blocked the sunlight, but she refused to let him know he intimidated her, even when she backed herself against the wooden fencing guarding the resort's equipment.

Chance merely stepped close and penned her in. She looked up past his broad chest, his tanned throat, past his full, sensuous mouth and into his dark, hooded gaze. She didn't know if it was the early hour or the intoxicating scent of him, but her brain sent mixed signals.

Wrap your arms around him.

Run like hell.

He'd clearly just come off the mountain, maybe from a ride. His black biking shorts and matching damp shirt clung to every inch of him, and every inch was pretty amazing. No fancy gym body for this man, no his came custom-made from his lifestyle. Still, it was his eyes that drew her now, those fathomless eyes.

Both she and Chance had pointedly ignored what had happened between them. They'd both danced around the fact that if they so much as touched each other, they would most likely implode.

And yet he was nearly touching her now. Slowly, he took his gaze on a leisurely stroll down her still wet body, taking in her messed up hair, the borrowed jacket, the shorts...her bare legs.

And despite the fact that she was dressed quite modestly, the way he looked at her left her feeling...naked. "Good morning," Ally said, meaning to sound upbeat and confident, as if he didn't affect her at all, but her soft, whispery voice betrayed her.

"Morning." His voice wasn't any more steady than hers, which was interesting.

And unnerving.

Nothing new. They'd been playing this casual game for weeks now.

"Busy day," she noted.

He simply nodded and bit into the middle finger of his cycling glove and tugged it off. Then did the same with the other. He tossed them to the ground and planted his hands on the wood fence behind her head. "Were you on the river?"

He spoke so evenly. She would never have guessed at the bad temper behind that casual voice—except for the heat of it in his eyes. "Tim was showing me how to kayak."

"I thought you weren't a strong swimmer."

"Tim was right there."

"Stay out of the river, Ally."

"I don't respond well to demands."

"Too bad. Stay out of it. And suppose you tell me why you're wearing my jacket."

"*Your* jacket?" She shook her head. "No, Jo gave it to me to borrow."

"Yeah, from my office closet."

"I—" His eyes were dark and unreadable as ever, and she bit her lip, thinking she would have to kill Jo personally. Slowly. "I didn't know."

"Now *two* of my jackets will smell like you."

It embarrassed her that she had thought she'd been so independent here, and hadn't been at all. "Nothing a little detergent won't fix." Frustrated, she ducked from beneath his arms and went to pull off Jo's— his!—jacket. It was a pullover, with wide bands of rubber around the neck, waist and wrists, to keep out the water.

The bands also kept her in. Darn it, but it was hard to get off. She wriggled and writhed and pulled, but all that happened was she got caught, her arms up and over her head, the jacket holding her locked in that position.

She wriggled and writhed some more, but it was no use, she was good and truly stuck. "Um...Chance?"

He said nothing, but now that the jacket was over her face she couldn't see him. Great. With as much dignity as she could muster, she tried to escape again.

To no avail.

She really hated to have to ask him for anything, especially help. But she had trussed herself up like a pre-packaged chicken. "Chance?"

"Yeah." He sounded like he was strangling.

"Do you think you can help me pull this thing off?"

A long second later, she felt his hands on her. Her waist, then her shoulders as he tugged on the material. Beneath the jacket she wore the top of her two piece bathing suit, which meant he had to touch her bare skin. By the time he freed her, she had goose bumps over her entire body and it wasn't from the cold morning air.

Chance tossed the jacket down next to his gloves, his blue eyes touching her everywhere.

"Thanks." She backed up a step. "I'm sorry about—" Her words ended abruptly when he followed her, once again trapping her against the fence.

"I'm...um...pretty busy right now," she managed, her breathing coming in funny little pants.

A wicked smile lit his eyes and one corner of his mouth lifted as he studied the way her breathing made her breasts lift and fall. "Busy doing what, Prim?"

Trapped within his arms, she felt like a butterfly about to be pinned alive. Then, when he leaned closer still, so that his shirt brushed her nearly bare chest, so that only a breath of air separated their mouths, she felt more like a sacrificial lamb.

A willing one.

That mouth of his barely, just barely, brushed hers. "What are you busy doing?" he repeated softly.

She'd forgotten. Her entire world slipped away when he was near her like this. He turned her inside out, and knowing that, knowing he was amused by it, gave her the strength to turn her head to the side. "Work...stuff. I'm busy doing work stuff."

He slid his warm, work-roughened fingers under her jaw and brought her back around. His eyes went to her mouth and she thought—hoped, wished—that he might kiss her anyway.

"You're cold."

"No, I'm—" She bit back her sigh of pure pleasure when he cupped her cheeks in his big, warm hands.

His eyes were positively wicked. "Anything else you need warmed up?"

Oh boy. "N-no."

He lowered his gaze to her breasts, zeroing in on the way her nipples were pressing against the material of her bathing suit, and she wanted to punch him for making her stomach leap in anticipation. Instead she put her hands to his chest, meaning to push him away, but she felt the bunching of his muscles and the quick leaping of his heart, and knew that he was as affected by their closeness as she. If she moved, shifted a bit, his body would rub against her. Unable to help herself, she did just that, and encountered full contact.

He was completely aroused.

She raised her gaze to his face and found him looking back at her from beneath lowered lashes.

"I've been this way since you got here," he said.

She winced in sympathy. "I'll just...go then."

"I meant since you came to Wyoming."

Her eyes flew wide. "Oh. *Oh.*"

"Yeah, oh." For a moment he stayed close, then backed up imperceptibly. "You've got a message from home."

Thinking had become nearly impossible. Her heart was racing, her brain seriously impeded by the rush of blood from her head to all her erogenous zones. "My sisters again?"

"Yes." He cocked his head to the side. "Dani said

don't forget next Tuesday is Maggie's party. Come early and give her a hand, she said."

"Oh."

"You use that word a lot."

She'd already told her family she wouldn't get back that soon, but obviously Dani had wanted to pressure her, not realizing Ally could no longer be pressured.

"When were you going to tell Lucy?" he asked. "After you'd left?"

She pulled away because she couldn't think when they were touching. It was hard enough when he was merely standing in front of her, all tall, intense and attitude-ridden. "Why does it matter to you?"

His eyes glittered dangerously. "It doesn't. I happen to want you, yes, but it makes no difference to me whether you stay or go."

"You...want me?"

"Don't let it go to your head. I want a lot of women."

"Oh, man, I *really* don't want to hear this."

Both Chance and Ally turned in unison to face a scowling Brian. He stood there wearing jeans five sizes too big, and a shirt that went to his knees. His tattered bike leaned against his hip.

Chance was still looking at Ally with heat, frustration and promise, and she had no idea what any of it meant.

I want a lot of women.

She had no doubt of that. Or that he'd find those women with one crook of his finger.

It makes no difference whether you stay or go. Ally tried to let that roll off her back and failed.

Brian thrust out his chin toward Chance. "Riding today?"

With annoying ease, Chance changed gears. "Already did, Slick. What happened to school?"

He got the Brian shrug. "Stupid assembly."

Ally struggled to shift with the conversation. She knew Chance wasn't the type to be held by the rules of society. But she hoped to God he knew enough to send this kid back to school. Brian desperately needed to learn to live by the same rules as everyone else, and she was certain he wouldn't ever learn that from Chance, a man who'd never followed the rules at all.

Not that she was trying to save him, of course. Or anyone. But she couldn't stop the thought. *Please, don't be reckless with Brian.*

Chance looked at her, and as if he'd heard her thoughts, he went still. There'd been a heat in his eyes every single time he'd looked at her, from the very first day, from that very first moment she'd stepped off the plane. That heat had *always* been there, and it'd only gotten stronger as the days had passed.

Yet now, right this minute, it...died.

"Maybe we can take another ride. Off trail this time," Brian said into the charged silence.

"You're not ready." Chance was still looking at Ally with a disturbing lack of...anything.

It makes no difference to me... His words echoed in her head, but she pushed away the hurt because he'd never mislead her.

She'd mislead herself.

"I *am* ready," Brian insisted. "That last ride we took, we raced down. You showed me how to get the most speed out of it, remember?"

"I also showed you how to do it without killing yourself," Chance said. "Do you remember that part?"

"Yes. But—"

"No buts. Takes practice to be better than good."

"You said I was."

"Compared to any other fourteen-year-old, you are. You know that. Be different. Get *better* than good. And get to school. Only idiots ditch."

"Don't need school to be a pro boarder. Or a biker. Don't need school for any of that."

"Wrong," Chance said firmly, looking ticked. "Trust me on this one, you gotta finish high school to become a professional anything."

"Who says?"

"*I* say."

Brian shrugged and amazingly enough, headed toward the parking lot instead of back on the trail.

Chance shot Ally one last undecipherable look before he walked away.

"You're not going to your office?" she asked his back.

He shrugged, mirroring Brian's attitude, and kept walking.

With no idea why, she followed him, though she had to run to keep up with his long-legged stride. "What's your problem?"

"What makes you think I have one?"

"Because you won't even look at me."

He stopped so short she nearly plowed into the back of him. Her hands came up automatically, sliding over the sleek, taut muscles of his back. She snatched them back.

"I'm looking at you now," he said, turning to face her.

He was...*hurt*, she realized with shock, when she was the one who should be hurt. "But why are you looking at me like *that?*"

"Drop it."

In her not-too-distant past she might have meekly let it go, but she was no longer a mouse. She was big, bad, strong Ally who did as she pleased, when she pleased. "Tell me."

Temper flashed in his eyes. "I saw you, Ally. I heard your thoughts as if you'd screamed them. You actually thought I would let Brian do whatever the hell he wanted. Ride recklessly, ditch school, whatever. You seem to have this preconceived notion of me and how I live my life, and I don't like it."

"At least you have to admit, you live up to it."

He stepped close. "There you go again, assuming you know me."

Refusing to back up, Ally kept her eyes on his. "Then help me know you, Chance."

Lifting his hands, he shoved his fingers through his hair. The muscles in his arms were taut and strained. "This lifestyle is not for everyone. It's...dangerous."

"Are you trying to scare me off? Is that your new

tactic to discourage me?" She laughed. "I'm not very frightened."

"You should be," he growled. "This kind of life can cost you big."

There was something more than temper in his gaze now, but even as she watched him back away from her, all emotion—and *pain?*—vanished behind hooded, watchful eyes. Her stomach knotted, because this man, this brooding, edgy, dangerous man, drew her as no other ever had, and despite everything, she wanted to know him. "How can it cost, Chance? What has it cost you?"

"A friend." He paused and his voice lowered a fraction. "A close friend."

"What happened?"

"She underestimated the elements and it cost her everything. Her life," he said flatly.

She. Ally's stomach knotted again.

"I know you think I'm wild and out of control, but I have more control than you'll ever know. If I didn't, I'd have had you by now—and circumstances be damned."

She actually had to lick her lips and clear her throat to talk. "Circumstances?"

"Yeah." His eyes went hard. "You're leaving, remember?" Then he turned and walked away before she could tell him she wasn't going anywhere.

Not yet.

CHANCE HAD KNOWN she'd leave eventually. All along, it'd been what he'd wanted.

So why did he feel so empty?

"What's your problem?" Jo asked, when he'd been sitting at his desk, brooding, staring out the window for thirty minutes.

"Nothing. Where's Ally?"

"Ah." She let out a secret smile.

"What the hell kind of answer is that?"

She just grinned. "Why do you want to know where she is?"

To wring her neck. "Why do you keep answering my questions with more questions?"

"It amuses me."

"I need her," he said tightly. "We have work to go over."

"Uh-huh. Hard to do that with your lips locked." And at the look on Chance's face, she roared with laughter. "Well, *you're* the one thinking it, not me." Having pity she patted his arm. "And you ought to know, I didn't figure this one out entirely by myself. Brian helped. You've got the 'hots for her,' I think he said."

He let out an expletive.

She laughed at him some more. "Try rentals. Oh, and you might want to hurry."

"Why?"

"You'll see."

CHANCE DID INDEED find Ally in rentals, arranging to rent a kayak for the rest of the afternoon. *"What are you doing?"*

She fumbled with the helmet she'd thankfully put

on correctly, blew the hair out of her face and didn't answer him. When she hoisted the kayak and went outside, he followed, amazed at her strength. Her bare arms were tanned and toned with muscle. So were her legs. Gone was the fragile, vulnerable woman he always imagined her to be.

When exactly had *that* happened?

"Ally, I asked you a question."

"Go back to your cave, Chance."

He took the kayak from her and put it on the ground. "You don't know what you're doing."

"Oh, I know what I'm doing. Tim's been giving me lessons all week."

He stared at her, wondering when his world had turned into a *Twilight Zone* remake. "I told you to stay out of the river."

"And I told you I don't take demands well."

"I thought you were leaving, going back for your sister's party."

"You thought wrong." Her eyes were completely void of temper now. "Look, I know you think I'm speaking in tongues when I say this, but I want to be a *real* manager. I'm *trying* to be a *real* manager. And despite the fact that we'll never get along the way I want to, I'm smart enough to know you're the best person to teach me."

Well damn if that didn't both defuse his temper and humble him to the bone. Unable to help himself, he lifted a hand to her face, using his fingers to tuck her hair better into the helmet. At the feel of her smooth, soft, precious skin, he felt that now familiar ache from deep within him. He couldn't seem to stop touching her. Nor kissing her, apparently, because he leaned in, cupped her jaw in his hand and put his mouth against hers.

She kissed him back, slipping her fingers into his hair at his nape, drawing him closer, deeper, and when she made a sound of pleasure and desire mixed in one, he was lost. He might have stayed that way forever, locked in her arms, if the smell of smoke hadn't finally penetrated his swamped senses.

Smoke.

He looked up and his heart nearly leaped right out of his chest. Above them, the summit once again raged with flames.

8

WITHIN AN HOUR they had ground support, air support, and more of both on the way for the flare-up. There were firefighters on the backside of the mountain, digging their way through a firebreak, and more on the west and east side, attempting to gain quick control this time.

Ally watched Chance quickly and methodically make sure every guest and employee was safe and accounted for. She witnessed his anguish, his fear, and felt it as her own.

"All staff members on duty are on the radio," Ally told him as she caught up with him in his office. "They're just waiting for directions."

"The only direction is to stay the hell out of danger and let the firefighters do their thing." He shouldered his backpack, checked his radio and headed toward the door.

He was going up there, she realized with a shock. She grabbed his arm. "What happened to staying out of harm's way?"

"I'm going to see what's going on."

"No!"

A pained look crossed his strong features. "Ally, standing down here, over a mile away, torturing myself with what's happening to the land, *again*, is killing me." Abruptly, he shrugged her off. "I'll radio you with whatever news I get."

"No! Stay here, stay where it's—"

"Safe?" He whirled on her, eyes hot and fierce, jaw tense. "Not if there's anything I can do to help." Then, shocking her further, he kissed her, hard, and on impulse, she clung to him.

For just a moment, he clung back.

"Be careful," she whispered.

Without another word, he vanished out the door.

ALLY'S HEART REMAINED firmly in her throat, until the fire was fully contained and everyone was safe and accounted for.

Including Chance.

By midnight, things were finally quiet again. That was the good news, but there was bad as well. The fire chief didn't think the fire was a flare-up of the old one, which meant it could either be the unusual heat wave or arson, and they'd be looking for answers come daylight.

Just the thought had Ally burning with fear and fury. It wasn't Brian, she knew that much. She'd witnessed his joy in this place. It had become his home. He wouldn't hurt it.

She turned off her office light, intending to go to her cabin and collapse in bed, but a light down the darkened hall drew her.

Chance.

All thoughts of sleep vanished, replaced by images

of comforting him, holding him close, somehow making him accept the fact that for once, *she* could help *him*. Even if that help came only in the form of comfort.

She was just outside his office door before she heard his low, quiet voice say, "Yes, everyone's safe."

"And Ally," came Lucy's voice from the speakerphone on his desk. "How's my Ally?"

Chance was leaning on his desk, arms crossed, staring out the windows into the dark night. Every inch of his body looked tense and taut as steel. As if he sensed her, he turned to the door. Their gazes met and locked. "Ally's okay," he said, staring at her. Absorbing her.

"And you?" Lucy asked, blissfully unaware of the tension now shimmering in the room. "I know you too damn well, Chance. You'll be the one out there where it's not safe."

Chance didn't break eye contact with Ally. "I'll be fine. I have to go, but I'll call you first thing in the morning, okay?"

"Fine. But Chance?"

"Yeah?"

"I love you, as if you were my own son. I just wanted you to know that."

CHANCE TURNED AWAY from the window and grabbed the phone. With his throat suddenly tight, so tight he could barely speak much less breathe, he was eternally grateful for the dark room.

"Say it," Lucy said in his ear. "You don't have to tell

me you love me back, just say you know *I* love *you*, and that you believe it."

His eyes burned, and it wasn't from inhaling smoke for hours. "Lucy."

Her voice softened. "Hon, I know damn well you've never let your own family close enough to tell you how they feel, so let *me* tell you tonight of all nights, when things are as bad as they can get. Everyone needs that, needs to know they're loved."

He hadn't ever believed that, until now, but he couldn't speak past the football-size lump in his throat. He was painfully aware of Ally watching him.

"Chance? I'm going to keep telling you, do you hear me?"

"Hard to miss it," he managed gruffly. "You're shouting."

Although he knew Ally could no longer hear Lucy's side of the conversation, he saw her smile. It was a bit ragged, as was she from the night's events, and more than anything, he wanted to hold her. "I've really got to go."

"Okay, you don't want to talk mushy, I understand. But I meant what I said." Lucy's voice was full of warmth and affection. "Goodnight, Chance."

"Goodnight...and Lucy?" He waited until the last possible second to say it. "I love you, too."

He hung up and stared at the phone for a long moment before lifting his head. Ally was still there, silhouetted in the dark, open doorway. She was filthy, smelled like smoke, was pale as a ghost, and she'd never looked more beautiful to him. He wanted her, probably more than he'd ever wanted anyone, but that wasn't what scared him now, as he'd felt that need before, with other women. It was how badly he wanted to bury his face in her hair, wanted *her* to hold *him*, while together they rode out this terrible, haunting sense of...aloneness.

That was entirely new.

"You okay?" she asked, her voice soft and somehow comforting in the dark.

"You should be in bed." Another image he didn't need, her in a bed, all tangled in the silky sheets, hair spread over the pillow, lips soft and inviting...

"I'm going soon."

Good. Great. He'd be picturing that for the rest of the night. "Tired of the big, bad wilderness yet?"

"I miss the city," she admitted. "But I'm not tired of Wyoming."

Which wouldn't hold her here. He knew that.

"And to be honest..."

No, don't be honest, he wanted to say. *Don't open up to me. Don't make me care any more than I already do.*

"In the month before I came..." Her eyes flickered with embarrassment. "I managed to mess things up. I...lost my job when they accused me of stealing."

"You wouldn't do that."

"No," she agreed softly. "I wouldn't. But Thomas didn't have such qualms, and—"

"Thomas?"

"My very ex-boyfriend. He stole some classics and let me take the blame. Luckily he's the one that ended up in prison."

Chance was surprised at the hot white surge of fury that caused within him. "Doesn't sound like a good enough punishment to me."

To his surprise, she laughed. "It worked for me, once I got Lucy's letter asking me to come to Wyoming."

He gave in to the curiosity he'd been fighting. "Jo says your family calls a lot. Are you supporting all of them?"

"Does Jo always tell you about other people's private messages?"

"When she's worried about a friend."

Now it was Ally's turn to grimace. "She doesn't consider me a friend."

It surprised him, the look of hurt. And knowing he'd put most of it there made him uncomfortable. "I know that at first the staff wasn't exactly welcoming, but I also know that's changed."

"Uh-huh."

"Look, you work hard, you're good to everyone, and you genuinely care about this place and what we're doing. Any of them would do just about anything for you, you've got to know that."

She stared at him, her eyes suspiciously bright, and he groaned out loud.

But she quickly lifted a hand. "No, I'm okay. Really." She sniffed and shot him an embarrassed laugh. "But they like me? They really like me?" She swiped at a tear. "I like them, too, very much. And despite not wanting to..." She moved toward him now, oh God, right toward him, with a soft, warm light in her gaze. "I like you, too, Chance. A lot."

He didn't want to know this, and yet in a sick way, he *did* want to know it. *Sleep*, he decided. He needed sleep. That was all it was, just plain exhaustion.

Halfway convinced, he straightened away from the desk, but all that did was bring him into closer contact with the woman he couldn't get out of his head.

Sweet and fiery. Shy yet sexy. Smart as hell, but somewhat naive. Adventurous. Ally was all those things, and every one of them drove him crazy.

"You know all about me," she whispered, lifting a hand to his jaw. "But you never talk about yourself."

Her touch set his body on fire. "Not everyone is an open book."

She didn't take the bait and back off. Antsy Ally was learning to stand up for herself, and damn if that wasn't arousing all in itself.

"You're not afraid of a little conversation, are you?" she murmured, dancing her fingers across his skin.

He might have laughed at that open dare, but she was still watching him so intently. Curiously. She really wanted to know about him.

"Tell me about you, about *your* family," she pressed.

"I have one," he said.

"Ooh, three whole words about yourself."

"Very funny." He grabbed her hand so she couldn't touch him. "You already know everything. My parents are world travelers. They live in Las Vegas now. And I have two older brothers. Remember?"

"Yes... So you're the baby of the family." She smiled at that. "Hard to imagine. Do you see them often?"

"No."

"Why not?"

"Are you sure you're not tired? Because you look tired."

"Why not?" she repeated patiently.

"They're busy."

"Would you be there for them if they needed you?"

"You mean would I send them money for a summer wardrobe?" He laughed when she rolled her eyes. "No. But yeah, I'd be there if they needed me."

"And what about the friend who died? Were you married to her?"

"No." When she continued to look at him questioningly, without censure or morbid curiosity, just a genuine need to know about him, he sighed. "Tina and I were young and stupid, and thought we were in love."

"She...loved you." The words were softly spoken, so softly he had to lean close to hear. A strand of her hair clung to the stubble on his jaw. "And you loved her."

"Yes," he said, then hesitated. "At least I thought so at the time, though I never told her. But now..." Now the truth was, he wasn't so certain. Tina had been sweet and lovely, but so damn needy and vulnerable, despite her efforts to prove otherwise. Now he couldn't imagine loving the woman she'd been, and it made him sad. "I don't know," he said quietly.

"I understand," she whispered, putting her hand on his chest again. "I've been fooled by my heart."

"Thomas."

"Yes."

"He hurt you."

"And you've been hurt, too."

"Yes," he admitted, then shook his head. "I have no idea what it is about you that makes me tell you things."

"Because it's nice to be talking instead of circling each other, or—" She bit her lower lip and looked at him from beneath her lashes.

"Or...?"

"Kissing," she whispered.

"You don't like the kissing?"

"Oh, I like the kissing." Her gazed dropped to his mouth. "Too much."

"But? I'm sure I sensed one at the end of that sentence."

"But...we're different."

Unable to keep his distance, he stepped even loser. Their thighs bumped. "I tried to tell you that."

"I'm slow and careful—"

"I wouldn't say careful exactly," he interrupted.

"And you're fast and reckless."

"I assume we're not talking about sex." Chance heard his voice go rough with desire, all the more so when she sucked in a shaky breath. He still didn't touch her with his hands, though he itched to. Their bodies were straining toward each other, only a whisper apart. He could smell her, could feel her soft breath, and the warmth of her skin. "Because believe me," he murmured in her ear. "I like it slow *and* fast. Steady *and* reckless. I like it any way at all."

Her eyes sort of glazed over at that, and she licked her lips. "I'm...not talking about *that*. I meant knowing how different we are, it's hard to imagine... anything between us. Other than..."

His hands went to her waist, slowly slid around and up her spine. "*Sex*," he finished for her.

"Yes, well." She blushed. "I'm pretty sure that would work just fine."

It was a mistake, but in spite of smelling like fire, in spite of the grime clinging to both of them, he plowed his fingers through her hair from beneath, holding her head in his palms. He could tell by the way she was staring at him, wide-eyed, lips tremulous and open, that she wanted him to kiss her. He lowered his face. "Let's find out," he suggested against her lips.

"I...I—"

He slid the tip of his tongue over the seam of her mouth and she moaned. "I think that would be playing with fire." She pressed her hands to his chest. "And then there's all those other women you're wanting." Her eyes had gone solemn. "I don't like to share, Chance."

She was waiting...*hoping*, he'd say something more. Maybe even offer her some sort of commitment to go with the sex they both wanted so badly that they were shaking. She was wondering if maybe he could change, change for her, and his heart clenched hard.

He couldn't. Wouldn't.

"Chance..." Slowly, eyes on his, she kissed his jaw. His heart leaped. "Stop."

She kissed the corner of his mouth.

"If I touch you now," he said in a voice so thick and grainy he hardly recognized it, putting his hands on her hips to hold her away. "I won't stop. I won't stop until I've pulled off all our clothes, until I've touched and licked and kissed and sucked every inch of you."

Her mouth fell open.

"I won't stop until we're both mindless with it, completely gone, until there's nothing else. Do you understand what I'm saying, Ally?"

She only blinked and stared at him.

Chance was so turned on by his own images that he'd probably explode with just one kiss. "I'm saying you have to stop looking at me like that or it's going to happen, no ties or promises attached. I'm saying you should turn and run like hell."

She stared at her hand on his chest. Slowly she slid it over him, from one side to the other, and with each pass over his heart, the poor sucker doubled its workload. "I don't want to run." She lifted her gaze to his, daring. "Why should I? Because you're too big and tough for me? Well guess what? I'm pretty tough, too."

"Not tough enough," he said. Then, because he was close to doing something he'd never done before, because he was close to begging a woman, he turned and walked away. It wasn't until he was alone in his bed that he realized the truth.

She *was* tough. Far tougher than he.

9

THE FIRE INSPECTOR found empty soda cans, food wrappings, and a science text book near the origination point of the fire. The book just happened to come from the school Brian attended.

And Brian had been on the mountain yesterday.

He'd also been unsupervised for a great part of the afternoon, not to mention his sullen attitude when Chance tried to talk to him about it.

To Ally's horrified shock, the boy refused to either defend himself or give them an alibi for his whereabouts.

They sat in the lodge, on the main floor. Ally, Chance, the fire chief, the fire inspector, Jo and the very quiet Brian, all around one of the huge tables they used to feed their lunch crowds.

"Brian, *please*." Ally came close to him, put her hand on his arm and tried to reach him. "Please, just tell them you didn't start the fire."

His face defined defiance. "And you'll believe me, right?"

"Yes, I'll believe you."

He stared at his feet, stubbornly mute.

"I *will*. We'll all believe you." She looked up into

Chance's eyes, silently begging him for help. "Won't we?"

For once, his expression was free of teasing humor or that contagious wild heat, but instead, filled with everything he was feeling, fear leading the way.

Big, bad, wild man T. J. Chance was afraid.

And all Ally could do was tuck her hands in her pockets, because this wasn't her problem, her fight. She wasn't supposed to care.

But she did, so very much.

"Just tell the truth, Brian." Chance's voice was quiet and direct. "That's all we're asking."

"But you already know where I was yesterday. On the mountain. Remember? You were annoyed to see me. Just like you always are."

Chance closed his eyes. When he opened them again, they were filled with regret. "Do you know *why* you annoy me?"

"Yeah. I'm always in your way."

"Because you remind me of myself when I was young and looking for trouble."

Ally watched, heart in her throat. She knew Chance now, whether he liked it or not. She understood the wanderlust ways of his childhood. Understood the pain that the lifestyle had brought him later on with Tina, and the loss. He'd ended up here, and this was his home now. He'd learned, if not to love again, then at least that life didn't have to be all loneliness.

But how to explain that to a teenager who'd never known anything else?

"It's not annoyance I feel when I look at you,"

Chance told him. "And I'm sorry I let you think it. It's remorse. Worry."

Brian stared at Chance. "You...worry? About me?"

"More than you'll ever know."

Brian absorbed that for a moment. "But you had a billion other punks out there on the mountain yesterday. You're not bugging any of them about the fire. It's because you think I started the last one, and I didn't." His voice lowered to a mere whisper. "I really didn't."

A muscle jerked in Chance's jaw as he rose and walked around the table to Brian. He brushed past Ally and sat next to the boy then took Brian's shoulders in his hands and looked at him eye to eye. "I believe you, Brian. And you know what else? Everyone here that's worked with you? Everyone you've spoken to or done something for? We know you now, we see how happy you are here, and we *know* you wouldn't do this." Chance's gaze didn't leave Brian's as he clearly tried to convey the seriousness of the situation, tried to convince Brian to cooperate. "But the inspector *doesn't* know you, only your reputation, which is going to haunt you for a while yet, no matter how you've changed."

With heartbreaking intensity, Brian soaked up every word. "I have changed."

"I know. I know, Slick. So help us out. Help us help you."

Brian's gaze revealed his fear, his insecurity, and Ally wanted to cry. How many times in his life had someone stood behind him? Promised to back him up? And meant it?

Probably never.

In comparison, her life had been a piece of cake. But not Chance's. No matter how he tried to keep his distance, she could see the truth, could see that he looked into that boy's eyes and saw a kindred spirit that broke his heart.

It was another crack in to the wild man image, another insight into the complicated man that was T. J. Chance.

"Please, Brian," Chance urged softly.

Brian swallowed hard and in that moment, Ally was so certain he hadn't started that fire, *either* fire, that she would've staked her very life on it. He loved this place as much as she did, and probably for many of the same reasons. Here, unlike any other place on earth, he'd found he belonged. He was wanted, needed.

Here, he was home.

She waited for him to tell everyone that very thing.

"Tell the inspector," Chance said into the tense, silent room. "Tell him you didn't do it so we can get on with our day. We have to get out there on the hill and patrol the morbidly curious today, I know how much you want to help me do that."

But Brian's eyes shuttered, and Ally knew before he even spoke that he wouldn't defend himself.

"I have nothing to say," he said, not meeting anyone's gaze, especially Chance's. "Nothing."

BRIAN WASN'T CHARGED. There was no evidence, and while there might never be, Ally decided she couldn't take that chance.

She was going to take matters into her own hands.

She got herself a small backpack and filled it with snacks and water, more determined than she'd ever been.

"Where are you going?" Jo asked in surprise when they passed each other in the office hallway.

Where was she going? To completely override her own personal goals, apparently. She'd fallen into her old trap of saving the world, and she didn't care. Not when Brian needed her, not when she cared so much about him. Not when Chance needed her, too, though she doubted he would ever think so. But just looking at him, seeing his agony as he watched Brian, tore at her.

She'd mistakenly thought *she* needed *him*, that she needed his expertise, his strength. She'd been wrong about that, because here on this mountain, she'd found her own strength.

But maybe, just maybe, *she* could be needed, and not give up a piece of herself as she'd always let happen in her past. "I'm going up that mountain to check out the burn, and hopefully find something to clear Brian."

"What?" Jo looked horrified. "You can't do that."

"Of course I can. I'm worried sick."

"We're all worried sick, but I don't think you should—"

"He's innocent, Jo."

"Absolutely, he is, but..."

"But...what?"

"Well..." Jo bit her lip. "I don't want to insult you."

Ally had to laugh. "And when has that ever stopped you?"

"I just don't think you should go out there alone."

"You think it's dangerous?"

"Yeah," Jo said. "To your health."

"I'll stay on the trails. Really, this time." Ally reached out and took Jo's hand. "Brian's killing me, Jo. Already all his confidence and joy has vanished, just like that, just in one day." She was so afraid for him. His pride was gone, too. Even his swagger had disappeared.

"He refused to go riding with Chance this morning," Jo said softly. "They're both wrecked. We're *all* wrecks."

"So you understand."

"Look, give me an hour. I'll go with you, okay?"

"I can't wait. I'm afraid they're going to come back and charge him."

"Just let me page Chance." Jo raced into her office.

Though it was horribly rude, Ally took off. She had to, because she knew what Chance would do—go without her. If he hadn't already gone.

She had to do this.

She had a trail map and her determination to guide her, but all the same, when she stood on the lower mountain trail and stared up at the peaks, she hesitated.

It looked huge.

She wasn't stupid. She knew a month in the woods did not an expert make, but taking action felt good. And she wasn't alone, not really. There were people all over the place. The resort was open, business as usual despite the recent fire. There were bikers, hikers, patrollers...plenty of company.

Still, as she started, careful to stay precisely in the middle of the narrow trail that would lead to the summit, she heard and saw no one. Only nature. The sun beamed down on her, warming her gently, but she didn't look around much. She concentrated on her path. Though she hadn't yet come close to the fire site, her nose was assaulted by the scent of burn.

In no time, she was huffing and puffing, in spite of the workouts she gave herself every night in the lodge gym. She'd have sworn she'd covered miles already, but when she looked at her watch, seriously contemplating a break, she had to laugh.

She'd been on the trail for twenty minutes. Well, at least she was still on the trail. She took off again, but didn't get another twenty yards before a very familiar, achingly sexy voice sounded in her ear.

"What the hell are you doing out here?"

God, that voice. Her nerves went to town and she didn't want to acknowledge what her heart did at just the sight of Chance standing there, quiet and brooding, wearing those jeans of his that made her want to do wild and thrilling things to his body. He was also wearing that fiercely guarded expression, the one that was always mixed with a sort of bafflement when he looked at her, as if he wasn't quite certain how he felt about her.

Well, they were even there.

She wanted to soothe him, comfort him. Be with him. She knew how ridiculous that was, but it made it no less real. "How did you find me?"

"Jo radioed me about your disappearing act. You scared her half to death."

She crossed her arms. "I'm going to take that as an insult."

"You can take it any way you want."

"I'm perfectly capable of staying on the path and keeping out of trouble."

"You'll excuse me if I refrain from comment." He glanced at the map she held, eyes narrowed.

"I'm looking for clues," she told him, fully aware she sounded really...*dumb.* "I just wanted to do something." She lifted the map, blushing when she realized it was upside down.

He grabbed it, and turned it right side up and slapped it back in her hands. "It might actually be worth something if you look at it the right way. God, Ally." He looked at her in complete confusion. "Why do I always feel the need to lock you up somewhere?"

She couldn't hold back her smile. "Because you like me?" But her amusement faded at the thought of *why* they were both there. "Don't make me go back, not yet. I want to help Brian. I know you do, too."

Chance tilted his head up and stared into the startlingly blue sky, hands on his hips now in an aggressive, frustrated stance. "Honestly, with that kid, I'm running blind."

"You're doing okay."

"Somehow I just...understand him." He shook his head and looked at her. "And why in the hell do I keep ending up talking to you like this?"

Her heart clenched. "For the same reason I end up talking to *you*."

"Yeah? What's that? Insanity?"

"You must know by now," she said carefully. "How much I care about you."

"But...why?"

She lifted a shoulder and gave him a little smile. "Bad habit. I'm always caring when I shouldn't."

"And trying to solve everyone's problems."

"No," she denied. "I gave that up before I got here."

His lips quirked at that, though his eyes remained dark. Troubled. "Just don't try to solve *me*. And I'm sure Brian would say the same."

There were lines of exhaustion around his eyes, and tension in his entire body. She wished she could soothe both away, but that was silly. He didn't want comfort from her. He didn't want anything from her except maybe her exiting Wyoming.

"You had another call," he said.

"From Lucy?"

"No." He looked at her strangely. "From San Francisco."

"Oh, yeah." From "home." She seemed to keep forgetting that Wyoming wasn't where she belonged.

"It was Maggie." He watched her with a frustrated

heat and intensity that still, after all these weeks, made her knees weak.

What did he want from her? She hadn't a clue. She slipped a bottle of water out of her backpack and took a drink because she had no idea what to say or do. Closing her eyes, she let the warm sun dance over her face.

When he suddenly took her shoulders in his big, warm hands and turned her to face him, she squeaked in surprise. His jaw was doing that bunching thing, reminding her that no matter what he wanted her to believe, he *did* care.

His eyes were dark, so very dark, and before she could say a word, he captured her head in his hands, lifted her face and took her mouth.

With a thunk, her backpack hit the ground.

Her water hit next.

And he kissed her even harder, deeper, creating a delicious need she couldn't deny. She went instantly hot and trembly. Her body's immediate reaction both surprised and alarmed her because no one had ever done this to her before. No one but Chance, and she let out a sound that was pure heartfelt relief, wrapping her arms around him to wholly return the kiss, unable to think, unable to do anything but feel.

It was hot. Messy. *Glorious.*

He buried his hands in her hair, and when she did the same, he moaned from deep in his throat and pushed even closer, shoving a hard denim-clad thigh between hers, nearly making her pass out from the exquisite torture. Without breaking away, he gentled them both by nibbling at one corner of her mouth, then the other, tracing her lips with his tongue before sweeping it back against hers for another long, hot assault, devouring her. And his hands...they moved over her now, over her back, her bottom, then to her hips, his own rocking, grinding, bringing them both to a fevered pitch. She was drowning, she was dying, she was—

Blinking at him in shock when he abruptly pulled away and scowled at her.

"Dammit," he growled out, backing away from her as if she had the plague. *"Dammit."*

"What..." She had to clear her throat to speak. "What was that about?"

"Nothing. It was just a kiss."

Just a kiss.

That had been *just a kiss?*

Well she was certainly glad he'd cleared that up for her because she'd been quite positive it had been more, far more, as in something from the heart, from the soul. Her lips tingled, and she brought a hand up to them. They were wet, and aching for more. This was bad, very bad, because it wasn't just her body yearning for more, either. Nope, her heart hurt, too. And that's what scared her.

"I want to stay away from you," he said. "I mean to stay away from you."

"Well you're not doing a very good job."

"I'm going to try harder."

"Good. Because..." Her throat tightened. Just looking at him was bad for her mental health. She wanted him, plain and simple. And he wanted her, too; she knew that. But he didn't *want* to want her, and that hurt more than it should.

Suddenly she missed her old world. Her old, quiet world. Okay, maybe it hadn't been so quiet. Maybe she'd been too busy taking care of everyone but herself, but at least she hadn't hurt like this. "I want my old life back," she whispered.

He nodded curtly. "Then go get it."

So simple. So why, then, did it seem so hard?

10

CHANCE SPENT THE next few moments morosely watching Ally's all too nice behind as it wiggled its way farther up the mountain. She wore khaki shorts and a snug fitting T-shirt with a fleece vest. The material clung to her every curve in a way that made thinking a calculated effort. The insistent ache in his groin urged him to grab her back, beg forgiveness for being an insensitive jerk so that he could bury himself deep inside her and assuage this crazy need.

She wasn't speaking to him.

His only defense was that she'd kissed him stupid. Completely, utterly, one-hundred-percent *stupid.* Again.

I want my old life back. Her words echoed in his head. At least she knew enough to know she didn't belong here. From the moment she'd first gotten off the plane and looked at him with those huge eyes, she'd done nothing but complicate his life.

They were high up on the mountain now, on the edge of the burned acreage, where the fire had done the most damage. No longer did the fresh twigs crunch beneath their feet. Instead, the charred landscape gave way without a sound. Eerie, and infinitely sad.

He stood there on the line between the living and the dead, his senses assaulted by the acrid smell of smoke and burnt pine. In spite of their work up here, it would be years before the land repaired itself, and with a deep, unsettled sigh, he started moving again. "I have no idea what you think you're going to find."

Ally, looking as grim and shaken at the sight as he did, just kept walking, searching...all the while ignoring him. Which maybe, when he thought about it, worked in his favor. If she wasn't talking to him, wasn't looking at him, wasn't driving him crazy, then he couldn't ache for her. Soon Lucy would come back, Ally would go, and his life could return to normal. "Ally?"

She kept moving, head high, shoulders stiff, determination blazing from her every pore. God, she was something. Had he really ever thought her fragile? Vulnerable? Easily dismissed?

"Look!" she cried suddenly. "Look at this tree!"

It hadn't burned. The fire had leaped, sparing a square piece of land about twenty feet across. A little miracle.

What held her interest was a huge, old pine tree. Right at shoulder height was a spot bare of bark, where someone had carved it smooth. In the spot was an etched heart. And the initials B.H. + M.M.

"Brian," Ally whispered, reaching up above the heart where a blue scarf had been set. "Brian Hall." Spinning in a circle, she laughed, arms spread out wide. Then, in a move that completely shocked him, she flung herself into his arms and squeezed him tight.

She was soft and warm and smelled incredible, and his body reacted immediately, violently.

"It's perfect," she whispered, oblivious to his reaction. Still grinning, she pulled away. But when she caught him staring at her, probably with the hottest look of undisguised, unadulterated hunger she'd ever seen, her smile faded. Self-consciously, she tugged at her vest. "This must be where Brian and his secret girlfriend get together."

"You're reaching now."

"No, look. It rained two days ago, yet this scarf—*Brian's* scarf—is perfectly dry and clean, which means it had to be brought here recently, right? As in maybe even the day of the fire. That girl, whoever M.M. is, can provide an alibi for Brian."

"Maybe."

"Probably," she repeated stubbornly.

"It's not a bad make-out spot," he said, looking around at the thick trees, at the lush growth underfoot, all of which had been spared certain death by the firefighters. It was private, and he could imagine pressing Ally back against the tree, could imagine stripping her slowly, then burying himself between her soft thighs.

"It's definitely a spot for lovers." There was no mistaking her soft voice, her dreamy little sigh.

Which served as a vivid reminder that his prim little Ally wasn't so prim after all.

"Not that I condone them coming here," she said quickly. "They're far too young. But there's something magical, something—"

She broke off and shot him a quick glance before turning away, but it was enough to see the spark of heat, the slight blush to her cheeks. "Never mind." She slipped off her vest and kneeled on the ground, stuffing it in her backpack. Her hair fell over her face, and she was half turned from him, but there was no mistaking her emotions, which were all over her face.

Confusion.

A hunger to rival his.

And hurt.

It was the last that killed him. "Ally—"

"We'd better get back, it's a long walk."

"Brian's in school, or he'd better be," he heard himself saying. "We can ask him about the scarf later." He carefully removed it from the tree.

Still hunkered down by her backpack, she looked up warily. "Why would you want to stay here when you can hardly even look at me? You certainly can't *talk* to me. Or be friends with me the way you are with every single other person on your staff. In fact, if you're not yelling at me, you're—"

"I'm...?"

"Kissing me," she whispered. "You need to stop that. It just...messes with my head."

He found himself squatting beside her, reaching out to touch her arm. "It messes with mine, too."

"Then stop."

"I can't seem to do that." His fingers skimmed up her forearm past her elbow, passing lightly over her upper arm. She didn't so much as blink. *What was she thinking?* For once, he didn't have a clue. His fingers dallied at her shoulder, and she shuddered.

"When you touched me before," he said softly, in apology. "When you hugged me—"

"I shouldn't have," she interrupted. "It was silly, I was just happy, that's all. Forget it."

He wanted to see her smile again. He didn't understand it, or the need to be the one responsible for that smile. But then again, he'd never understood half the emotions she caused in him.

So he stopped thinking and acted, slowly standing, drawing her up as well. Their bodies were close, and he entwined one hand with hers. With his other hand, he gently slid the scarf over her cheek, her jaw.

Ally closed her eyes. She couldn't help herself. When he stroked her again, she made a sound that surely told him exactly what he was doing to her. "Don't worry," she managed. "Lucy will be back really soon."

"Yes."

"And I'm leaving."

"Yes."

She opened her eyes and lifted her gaze to his, and there was something so hot, so intense in the way he looked at her. Like he wanted to consume her, inhale her, devour her. But they weren't intimate. They weren't even friends. "You'll be glad when I go."

"Yeah," he agreed, in complete contradiction to the regret in his eyes. He touched her again.

Again she closed her eyes, needing to protect herself from that look, from the wonder and the heat and the affection, because it wasn't real, it couldn't be real.

He couldn't really feel those things for her. "You want to stay away from me, remember?"

"I can't," he said softly. The cool scarf slid over her neck now. His thighs brushed hers. His chest slid close too, in a touch so light she wasn't sure it was real. But her nipples hardened and her heart sped up. She gripped his fingers tight. "Chance..."

"When you touch me," he said, his voice as silky as the scarf, "I get instantly hard. Did you know that?"

"N-no—"

He rocked his hips to hers.

"Um...yes." He was most definitely hard.

He rocked again.

Very hard.

She felt the scarf through her thin, V-necked T-shirt as he slid it down further, over her collar bone. His eyes followed the movement with dark intensity as he skimmed it over a breast and the very turgid tip. Unable to contain her small gasp, she reached behind her and grasped the tree so that she didn't collapse. "Chance—"

"I want to taste you again," he murmured into her hair as he dropped the scarf and wrapped his arms around her.

"No kisses," she said quickly, trying to pull back, but he held her right where he wanted her, not hurting her, not letting her go, either. "Remember? We just decided."

He simply brushed his mouth across her cheek and

jaw, to the soft spot beneath her ear, where he gently drew in a patch of skin and sucked.

Was it possible for bones to melt? "Why are you doing this to me?"

"Because it feels good. You feel good." He brushed his lips over hers. "You taste good, too." And then he used his tongue, slowly, thoroughly. Expertly.

Instant heat. Instant need.

He angled her head where he wanted her and brought her against him, hard. At the feel of him, so wild, so aroused, she shivered. He simply drew her even closer, his hands sliding over her waist, her hips, her back, untucking her shirt so he could touch bare skin, and when he did, he moaned at the feel of her.

It was a struggle to remember they had no future. That he was determined to be alone to live as he chose. That she was determined not to mess up her life again. She didn't want to care for him, didn't want to care for *anyone* this way, at least not now.

She wanted her freedom, too.

But freedom didn't have to mean celibacy. She could want him, have him, then walk away, couldn't she? It could be part of the adventure. Knowing that, she let herself sink into how he made her feel. He was so good at making her aware of nothing but him, at making her skin hot, her mind blank. Making her want to do things she'd never thought of before. So she kissed him back with all she had, which was with far more emotion than finesse, but he didn't seem to mind. She couldn't stop touching him, running her hands over his corded neck, his broad shoulders, the hard planes of his chest and the bunched muscles of his arms.

With a low, heartfelt groan, he pressed her back against the tree. She felt his fingers stroke her sides beneath her shirt, outlining her ribs. His warm, calloused hands skimmed over her belly, tingling every inch of her heated, damp body. "So soft," he whispered. Nibbling his way to her ear, he let out a rough sound of pleasure as his hands closed over her breasts. His fingers were long and warm, and he glided his thumbs over her tight nipples, back and forth, making her whimper for more. One of his hands slipped down, down, past her bottom, her thighs, catching her behind the knee, lifting her leg up to his hip, so that he could press his hips to hers and glide the neediest part of him to the neediest part of her.

She nearly lost it. Her limbs turned to rubber, her vision was interrupted by stars and her head hit the tree trunk with a light thud as she cried out his name, so close, so close...

"I've wanted to touch you this way since I first saw you," he whispered against her ear.

Beyond manners, beyond rational thought, much less humility, she grasped his shirt in her fists. "Then touch me. Touch me now."

"Here?" he murmured, dipping his head to kiss her throat. He sounded as if he'd just gotten out of bed. Rough. Sexy.

Well, she'd wanted wild, hadn't she? And he was making her wild, no doubt. "Here."

His deep, dark gaze searched hers for exactly one

heartbeat before he lifted her shirt over her head and tossed it aside. With a flick of his fingers, her front-clasp bra opened and he took her aching flesh into his hands, making them both gasp with pleasure.

She tugged off his shirt, too. So far gone she didn't care that they had only the sky and the trees for coverage. At the sight of all his dark, edgy beauty, right here in front of her, all hot and aroused, for her, she nearly sank to the ground.

With no little amount of awe, she ran her fingers over hard muscle and hot skin that rippled with strength and quivered with desire at her touch. Marveling at the feel of him, she wanted more, and tried to get it. Bold for the first time in her life, she cupped him in her hands. He blew out a serrated breath and captured her wrists. Gathering them over her head against the tree, he looked down at her with a gaze so hot it sizzled her skin everywhere it landed.

"I want to touch you," she murmured, flexing against the restraint, letting out a sigh when he bent to trace wet, openmouthed kisses over the column of her neck.

He groaned when she arched against him, groaned again when she rubbed her aroused, aching flesh back and forth over his erection. "Not...yet."

Her protest ended on a shivery sigh as his lips closed over a nipple, sucking her into his warm, wet mouth, making her writhe against him, straining against the hand that still held her to the tree. His free hand slid down her body to the button at the top of her shorts. He lifted his head, staring into her eyes, and slowly undid it. Next came the rasp of her zipper. His fingers squeezed her waist, stroked the base of her spine, then skimmed lower, inside the material now, where he spread his hand wide over her bottom, kneading her bare skin, urging her to feel him, all of him, every single hard inch.

He still had her hands and gaze captive, but it was the subtle movement of his hips to hers that really held her bonded, and helplessly she thrust back, again and again, a slave to the erotic rhythm that only mocked what she really wanted. "Chance..."

"I know." He dropped to his knees before her, slipping off one of her shoes, then the other, his fingers lingering over her thighs and calves as he skimmed off her shorts as well.

Which left her standing outside in the bright morning sun, wearing nothing but an uncertain smile and white cotton panties. She'd forgotten that an adventuress would probably have invested in sexy lingerie.

He hooked his thumbs under the elastic.

Stricken with a sudden sense of modesty, she put her hands over his. *What was she doing?* She tried to pull him back up, but he was unbudgeable. "Um... Chance?"

He slowly tugged on the only scrap of material covering her.

"I'm thinking that maybe this isn't— *Oh, my,*" she gasped as his tongue swirled over her hipbone. "I'm not sure—" This time she broke off with a moan as he took a little bite out of her, but when she could draw a breath, she gamely tried again. "It's...a little breezy out here."

"I'll keep you warm," he promised.

Okay, he'd keep her warm.

Her embarrassment didn't stand a chance of maintaining itself, not when he slowly dragged her panties down, past her thighs, her knees...gone. He let out a moan at the sight of her, and his head bent to his task as he gently guided her legs farther apart so he could touch her with his fingers, opening her to him so that he could kiss her...*there.*

She let out a surprised cry that was actually little more than a whimper, and sank her fingers into his hair, thinking he shouldn't, she shouldn't— But his tongue stroked, claimed, teased, tormented and performed the most magical sweet torture she'd ever experienced.

And somehow she ended up tugging him closer.

Against her, he groaned and gripping her hips, holding her still while his greedy tongue took over her world. She trembled, she cried out, she went utterly, utterly still, holding back with every ounce of control she had.

"Come for me," he coaxed in the sexiest voice she'd ever heard.

"I can't," she said without thinking.

It was his turn to go still, and he looked up at her with dark, dark eyes. "You've never?"

"I— Well—"

"Ally?"

She closed her eyes, a light breeze dancing over her

bare skin, as she admitted the embarrassing truth. "Only...you know...by myself."

She felt him staring up at her. "Are you telling me Thomas never—"

She managed to look at him, blushing wildly under his intensely heated expression. "He was usually...in a hurry."

"And before him?"

"No one," she whispered.

Chance ran his gaze slowly over her very naked body, his eyes flaring with heat. "Since he was an idiot, and you're the hottest thing I've ever seen, let's surmise it was *his* failing, not yours."

"I don't know, I—"

"Trust me on this, sweetheart. Trust me. In fact, let me start all over...right here—"

Her breath caught at the barely there touch of his fingers on her skin.

"And here..."

His thumb was featherlight, and on the one spot that could make her instantly hot and trembly. "*Chance?*"

"Right here, Ally."

Such soft, slow strokes, she couldn't control the rocking of her hips.

"And this, what do you think of this...?" His fingers were magic, firmer now, and in a rhythm that matched her pulse, gliding in and out of her wetness, in and out...

At her low, needy cry, he let out a rough groan.

"Yeah, you like that. Come for me, Ally, come for me…"

That simply, she shattered. She would have fallen to the ground in a weak, trembling, boneless heap if he hadn't surged to his feet and caught her, holding her upright. Though she could hardly see, much less breathe, she blinked at him, stunned. Exposed. Aching and yearning.

"More," he whispered, "I want more of you."

"Yes," was all she could say, and then his mouth was on hers, his hands on her skin. She felt a blinding stroke of intense need, a need so violent she thought she would die if it wasn't met, even after the most mind-blowing orgasm of her life.

Unable to just stand there and receive, she tore at his jeans, fumbling, but it didn't matter. He helped her, and not nearly soon enough, his jeans were opened and a condom was in place. Lifting her off the ground, bracing her against the tree—*their* tree now—he sank into her, his quiet "oh yeah" echoing in her mind. She cried out his name, she couldn't help it, it was so powerful, the pleasure so perfect, all she could do was hold on for dear life as he filled her body, mind and soul.

"Wrap your legs around me," he commanded in a rough, thrilling whisper. "Like that, just like that." His hands weren't any more steady than hers, and it filled her with such a sense of feminine power, she nearly came again from just the look on his face.

Then he moved, oh how he moved. His big body pressed her into the tree as he thrust into her, pumping his hips until she quivered and shuddered, over and over again. Then he was coming, too, powerfully, triggering another helpless response from her.

Afterwards, he softly breathed her name as they slumped together against the tree. He was still holding her, and while his heart rate slowed, his mouth found the spot where her jaw and neck met.

Clinging to him for balance, Ally was dazed, sated and quite possibly glowing with satisfaction, especially when they stayed like that for a long, long time, together in a way she hadn't imagined possible. Then, eventually, he released her so that she slowly slid down his body, and sensitive as her flesh was, her body tightened again, at the mere feel of him.

He must have felt it, too, but still he pulled away, holding her steady until she stood on her own shaky legs. He found her panties, which had been flung over a branch, and helped her back into her clothing.

But he didn't speak to her, not once while they hiked down and showed Brian the scarf or when they got him to admit he had indeed been up on the mountain before the fire started, with his girlfriend, the same girlfriend he refused to name for reasons only he could possibly understand.

Chance didn't speak to her, not even when Brian's girlfriend came forward on her own, when she confirmed Brian had been with her the entire day, that he'd been protecting her from the wrath of her father, that they hadn't had anything to do with the fire.

He didn't speak to her at all.

CHANCE DIDN'T DO "love," only sex. But he'd had plenty of sex in his life, and nothing compared to what had just happened with Ally in the woods.

Against a tree. Lord. He'd known from the very first kiss it would be more than just a hot coupling, and still, he'd done it. Even knowing she wouldn't be able to turn back, that she'd expect more from him than just the physical release, he'd gone ahead and taken her.

He couldn't stop thinking about that, and the reasons why. Ever since he'd discovered women and the pleasures they could bring, he'd done his best to do two things. Always give the pleasure back, and make sure to keep everything on a temporary basis.

He had no doubt he'd done the first. He'd given Ally pleasure back. Her soft cries and low whimpers had assured him of that. The way she'd held him, stroked him, giving every bit as much as she got, had assured him, too.

But as far as keeping things temporary, he'd really screwed up. He didn't claim to know all Ally's private thoughts, but he could bet the bank she had taken their actions very seriously.

What now?

He could walk away.

He could take her again.

Definitely the walking away option was the kindest, but either way, the end result wouldn't change. She would leave Wyoming. She'd get her life back, and…so would he. But there would be hurt.

That had been the one thing he'd wanted to avoid at all costs, and it was now inevitable.

Damage control, he decided. He needed some serious damage control, and quick. Because that made him ache, made the heart inside his chest do a slow roll and a hard squeeze, he rubbed a hand there.

It didn't matter that he already hurt. He would just get over it. He'd get over it, and her.

11

ONCE AGAIN THEY ALL gathered in the lodge. Jo sat next to Brian and took his hand. Chance stood behind him and put a hand on his shoulder, his face a mask of strength and careful control.

No insight to his thoughts there, thought Ally in frustration. He'd hidden everything, and if he remembered what they'd been doing in the woods only a little while before, there was no sign of it.

And yet when their gazes met, his eyes flickered with that heat that made her knees quiver.

Okay, he remembered.

Then Brian looked up at Chance with an expression of nervousness and fear, and Chance sent him a small, reassuring smile, one that brought both a sheen of tears and a smile of hope to Ally.

See? she reassured herself. Tough as Chance was, his heart wasn't immune. And if it could accept Brian, maybe it could accept her as well.

She looked at the people she'd grown to care so much about and felt such a burst of warm emotion she could hardly speak. They were a unit.

And she was part of that unit. For the first time in her life, she belonged. Not because of what she could do or provide, but because she as a person was wanted and welcome. She needed them, and they needed her.

She *loved* that. She'd come for the adventure, was still here for the adventure, but contrary to what she'd once thought, she'd definitely be leaving a piece of her heart here when she left.

"Tell us," Chance urged Brian.

With a deep breath, Brian did just that. He and Monica had been together, carving their initials into the tree and "messing" around, leaving by three-thirty so she wouldn't get caught by her father. They'd been gone by the time the fire had started, at approximately four o'clock. He hadn't wanted to say so before because he hadn't wanted to get her in trouble, which she'd be bound for if her father had known the truth.

He'd been protecting the girl.

Ally's heart broke, but for the moment at least, Brain was free from more trouble with the law. She wanted to believe he'd been scared straight by the events, but she wasn't that naive. Whatever he felt was well hidden beneath his tough bravado.

The boy reminded her so much of Chance, and his equally tough bravado. But she'd seen past the facade now, and there was no going back.

If only either one of them would let her all the way in.

MUCH LATER SHE CAME across Brian. He was alone in the huge, deserted locker room in the lodge, staring at his opened locker. Just staring, all tough guy gone, just one lone teenager, unsure of his future.

Ally's heart twisted, and she stepped toward him, but it turned out he wasn't alone at all.

Down the aisle, about fifteen lockers away, stood an equally silent, an equally alone Chance.

Everything inside her reacted at just the sight of him. She thought she'd been quiet, but she must have given herself away somehow, because he turned his head and looked right at her. Though his eyes flared with some emotion she didn't dare place, he said not a word. *Hadn't* said one word directly to her since they'd ravished each other.

Her face flamed, but oddly enough, it wasn't embarrassment making her hot, but the actual memory of what they'd done. How it had felt. *Incredible.* She wanted to feel it—him—again.

But since she couldn't say so, she looked at Brian. "I don't know about you," she said quietly. "But I'm glad it's over. And I wanted to tell you how proud I am."

He lifted one shoulder, still staring at his biking helmet and gloves.

"You going for a ride?"

"I have work." He slammed the locker and started to walk away, only to stop before he got to the door. With his back to both her and Chance, he said, "You believed me. You always did." He turned then, and looked at her from eyes blazing with confusion and pain. "Why?"

That, at least, was simple. "Because I believe *in* you."

Brian's gaze shifted to Chance, then down to his

feet, which he shuffled around a bit. "Chance told me the same thing."

Ally looked at Chance, who held her gaze with an unreadable expression. "Then you know it's the truth," she said.

Brian's smile transformed his tough, hard face into what a fourteen-year-old's *should* look like. "Yeah." He shot a sideways glance at Chance. "You're not mad anymore because of Monica?"

"I was never mad because of Monica," Chance said.

"But she's the daughter of your competitor."

"You'll see who you want."

Brian ran his fingers over the helmet Chance had given him. "I thought maybe you wouldn't want me around anymore if you found out."

"You thought wrong."

"Yeah, well. Cool."

"Look, uh..." The big, uninhibited, overtly sexual Chance grimaced. "Do we need to have the birds and bees talk?"

"Jeez!"

"Do we?"

Mortified, Brian shook his head. "*No.*"

"Good. That's good." Chance's smile was all relief. "Let's ride."

"I have to pick up trash."

"You can do that afterwards."

Looking as if he'd won the lotto, Brian grabbed his gloves.

"Be safe," Ally called out, waving, but Brian was already gone.

Chance took his gear, shut his locker and moved toward the door, which meant he had to walk directly past her, in an aisle not quite wide enough for him to pass by without touching her.

Refusing to turn her back and make it easy for him, Ally held her ground and looked directly into his eyes as he turned sideways to go by her.

Their thighs brushed. His arm swept across the front of her. Though the touch was barely there, and in no way intentional, her body reacted.

And he could deny it until the end of time, but he wasn't unaffected either. He looked at her, and at the emotions blaring there she nearly cried.

"You okay?" he asked.

"Yes. I'm glad Brian's safe from trouble—"

"No, I meant about...before."

"You mean when we made love outside?" New life, new rules, she reminded herself. *Hold nothing back.* "Against a tree?"

He winced and raked his hands through his hair. "Yes. God, I've never felt like such a stupid teenager in my life. Not even when I *was* a stupid teenager." Swearing again, he put his hands on her hips and snagged her close. Then he cupped her face, stroking his fingers against her cheek. "Did I hurt you, Ally?"

That wasn't what she expected. And with him touching her, his voice low and grim with concern, she found herself speechless.

"Did I?" he demanded.

"No." A small, shy smile escaped. "Quite the opposite, actually."

Some of his intensity faded and his lips curved slightly. "Yeah?"

She smiled, and thought maybe she'd reached him then, maybe she'd gotten past that protective barrier, but he stepped back, robbing her of his warmth.

"You're sorry about what happened," she said bluntly, her voice not quite as strong as her resolve. "I thought it was usually the woman who had regrets. No, wait." She pressed her fingers to her eyes so that she didn't have to see that tortured look on his face. "I have no right to press you—"

"Chance?" Brian poked his head back into the locker room, his expression both eager and anxious. "Did you change your mind?"

Chance didn't take his eyes off Ally. "No, Slick. We're going. I just need a moment here."

But Ally didn't want to hear his regrets, didn't want to hear why the most amazing experience of her life could never happen again, so she turned away and smiled reassuringly at Brian.

Or she *hoped* it was a reassuring smile, and not the near-tears she really felt. "He's coming right now," she said. "He's all yours."

THE RIDE WAS GOOD, and so was Brian. He'd developed an amazing biking skill over the past few weeks, and damn if Chance wasn't growing fond of the obnoxious, surly, sour fourteen-year-old.

He was growing fond of lots of things lately. Things, and...people. One woman in particular.

He was showered, changed and standing at his office window, staring out at the mountains, seeing only Ally, and that light in her eyes that shone whenever she looked at him.

Then he caught sight of a kayak on the river and his heart all but stopped.

She was out there alone. Dammit, he was tired of saving her pretty butt. He wouldn't do it again.

He wouldn't.

But the kayak could tip, and he knew she wasn't a strong swimmer, and that the current was tough, and...and he raced out of his office, swearing, furious at both of them.

Running down the hallway, he skidded to a surprised halt at the doorway to her office, because there she sat behind her desk, on the phone, wearing not a bathing suit but a long, flowing sundress, covered with a million tiny flowers. Her hair was a little messy, as if she'd not given it a second thought all day, and he decided he liked that. Her lips were naked.

He liked that, too. He liked a lot of things about her, especially those little noises she made when he was deep inside her.

With a flick of his wrist, he locked her office door. At the startlingly loud sound of the lock falling into place, she faltered in midsentence, sent him a wide-eyed doe look that made him hot.

Still staring at him, she gripped the phone tighter.

Oh yeah, he already felt better. With a wicked smile, he pulled off his shirt.

Ally stuttered into the receiver, obviously struggling to maintain her side of the phone conversation.

Sending her a slow wink, he perched a hip on her desk. Just looking at her made him hungry for a taste of her, and he licked his lower lip.

Ally stared at his mouth, hers open, and dropped the phone. Blushing, she quickly picked it up, apologizing into it.

Enjoying himself immensely now, Chance leaned in and toyed with a strand of her hair. Then he stroked a finger over the very tip of her earlobe.

She abruptly rose and turned her back to him.

He simply stood behind her, slid his hand around her waist to her stomach and pulled her back against his already raging hard-on. Spreading his fingers wide, he touched as much of her as he could. His thumb brushed the underside of her breasts, then he cupped the soft curves. Her hard nipples pressed into his hands and he rasped his thumbs over them.

Letting out a choked sound, she stammered out some excuse, and finally hung up. Her cheeks were flushed, her hair messy, and she backed away from him, avoiding his gaze. "You're back from riding all in one piece."

"Yep. You look good enough to eat, Ally."

Suddenly she was the picture of busy; the piles on her desk, her filing, her computer. Anything and everything had her attention, except him.

Leaning back against her desk, he pulled her between his thighs. "Why are you so nervous?"

"I'm always nervous before I get dumped."

"Dumped?"

"Don't look so shocked," she said, searching his

gaze. "I know what you'd like to do to me. You'd like to ship me back to where I came from. Pretend I never showed up."

"No, actually, that's not what I'd like to do to you."

She blinked, then blushed. "Be serious."

"Oh, I'm being very serious."

She slowly shook her head and backed away from him. "Don't tease. Not about this. Just dump and go."

He didn't want to "dump" her. In fact, he wanted *more* of her, and he was even beginning to think maybe he could never get enough.

"Chance?" Her voice was tentative now. "What happened up there, between us? In the woods?"

He skimmed a finger up her arm, over her jaw and into her silky hair. "I was hoping you'd know."

She shook her head.

"I'm sure this is no surprise," he said softly. "But I'm not comfortable with what you make me feel."

She searched his gaze for a long, long moment. "I'm not comfortable with very much when it comes to you," she finally said.

"So we're even."

She seemed fascinated by his mouth, and he nearly groaned when she licked her dry lips. Blood drained from his head to parts south. He ran his thumb over her lower lip, but she caught his hand.

"Don't," she whispered. "I can't think when you do that."

"Thinking is overrated."

"Yeah?"

"Yeah." He pulled her closer, so that they were

touching from head to toe, and all the delicious hot spots between. His hips slid against hers, and she let out a dark, needy sound that inflamed him. "Do you want me, Ally?"

Against his throat, she moaned.

He skimmed his hands over her luscious, warm body, then back up again, beneath the material of her dress now, bending his head to kiss her neck because he couldn't get enough. He stroked the backs of calves, her knees. Her thighs, and when he discovered no stockings, no nylons, nothing but Ally, he nearly came right there.

She wrapped her arms around him and bit his neck. "You make me...wild," she whispered.

"Wild is good." He slid his fingers down, down, between her thighs, and found her hot and wet. "Do you want me?" he asked again, though he'd never asked a woman that before. He'd never cared that much, but he cared now. "Ally?"

"Jo is right outside—"

He stroked her with slow precision, nearly blind with need. "Yes or no."

"*Yes!*"

Scooping her up, he set her on the desk, stopping only to shove all the papers to the floor. By the time everything hit with a loud thunk, he'd scooped up her dress, slipped off her panties, fought with her fingers to get his jeans opened, and got a condom out of his pocket.

"Let me," she murmured, then bent to the task.

She didn't know what she was doing, and that in itself got him so hot and bothered he had to take over.

She tilted her head up and looked at him from sexy, sleepy eyes. "Am I doing it wrong?"

He could only let out a choked laugh. "No, you're doing it right. *Too* right." Pressing her thighs apart with his hands, he stepped between them and entered her. At the hot, wet feel of her, his knees nearly buckled.

"Oh, my," she whispered.

Definitely *oh, my*.

Gripping her hips, one stroke from bliss, he set his forehead to hers and forced himself utterly still. "Don't move, not yet."

"I can't help it." She arched against him, head thrown back, eyes closed, breasts thrust out, easily the most incredible sight he'd ever seen, and for a moment it was all he could do to just hold on.

He was lost. He was so lost. In her.

Her eyes fluttered open, glossy and filled with desire. "Chance..." Tenderly, she cupped his face, brought it down to hers and kissed him. Then she moved against him, bringing him even deeper inside her.

And suddenly, so close to her he had no idea where he ended and she began, he realized the truth.

He wasn't lost at all, and hadn't been since she'd stepped off the plane and into his life.

And soon enough, she was going to step right back out of his life.

12

THAT NIGHT, CHANCE came to her and they spent the hours until dawn attempting to quench their desire for each other.

It couldn't be done.

Ally realized it as the dark gave way to a streaky, gray morning sky, as Chance left her bed with a kiss and a husky promise to return that night, as she watched him go with both a yearning and a growing acceptance of her feelings.

She'd tried to escape it by saying this was just part of the adventure, that it was purely physical.

It was a lie.

But if she'd learned one thing on her wild adventure here in Wyoming, it was that her life was truly her own. She'd learned to believe in herself and her abilities. She'd learned to trust her heart.

And her heart was in love with T. J. Chance.

THE RESORT MIGHT HAVE been slow in opening for summer, but it got going with gusto. They had cabins rented. Bikers on the slopes. Hikers on the peaks. Kayakers on the river. Shops overflowing with happy shoppers.

And they were still understaffed enough to have

everyone overworked. Lucy was expected back any-time, and frankly that was a mixed blessing Chance didn't want to think about. But for the moment, the kitchen was low on food, First Aid needed supplies, and every other department was in need of something as well, yet no one could be spared to run to town.

No one but Chance, who enjoyed shopping about as much as he'd enjoy a hole in his head. Halfway to his Jeep, still grumbling, with no less than five different lists in his pocket, he came across Ally, who was just standing on the path, staring up at the huge mountain peaks, and the darkening clouds making their way over them.

Having finally climatized herself, she wore shorts and a white sleeveless blouse, with a sweater tied around her trim waist. Her legs looked long and toned and tanned, and good enough to nibble on. Her arms were nice, too, the results he'd discovered, from the time she'd spent in the resort's gym. He'd seen her there at night, in a crop top and snug shorts, pumping at weights, her skin damp and glowing. Often he'd gone back to his cabin and laid awake for hours fantasizing about her. But even more arousing was that she'd worked so hard to fit in, that she even wanted to. It no longer surprised him. What *did* surprise him was how he was standing there with a stupid grin and a sudden, undeniable erection, at the sight of her.

He was out of control.

She should have been out of his system by now. They'd certainly given it their best shot, against a tree, on her desk, in her bed—every which way imaginable.

And yet, still he wanted her.

She turned then, that just-for-him smile on her lips, her eyes lighting up at the sight of him, and the deep wanting became such a strong yearning he actually hurt.

"I was just thinking about you," she said softly. "About...last night."

Yeah, it was all over her flushed face, reflected in her gaze, and now that she'd turned toward him, caught by the morning light just right, he could see her nipples pressing against the material of her blouse.

His mouth went dry. Then drier still when she pressed her body to his and planted her mouth just beneath his ear. "I was thinking about all the things you did to me last night," she whispered.

Now he was, too, and he wondered if it was possible to pop open the buttons on his jeans with just a hard-on.

"I was thinking..." She took her mouth on a little tour of his jaw while his heart pounded in his ears. "That I'd like to lick you all over." She touched his mouth with just the tip of her tongue, then bit his lower lip.

He groaned, and gripped her hips hard, tempted to drag her off to the first semiprivate place he could find and let her have her way with him.

Out of control, a little voice whispered in his head. *You're out of control, needing her this way.* "There's a storm coming," he said gruffly, forcing himself to step back. He needed to back off, way off. "I'm going for supplies."

"Can I come?"

God, no. "Another time." He turned away from the far too welcome sight of her and walked to his Jeep.

She simply followed. "Why is it so hard for you to admit you might care for me, just a little?"

He opened the Jeep door and wondered why women all had to do this, had to analyze everything to death. "Dammit, I care for you."

"Well I know that. I'm just wondering why it's so hard for you to say so," she said simply.

Ignoring her, he got in.

So did she. "Afraid of something, Chance?"

He sighed, pinched the bridge of his nose and said, "This is a bad idea, Ally."

"Really?" She turned those huge, expressive eyes right on him. "You didn't think so last night when you tossed me onto my bed, took off my clothes and—"

"I remember," he said tightly.

"So why can we be so unbelievably intimate in the bedroom, but when it comes to outside of it, you shut me out?"

"I haven't changed."

She stared at him, then slowly shook her head, looking sad. "Then I guess it's me that's changed." She turned back to the window.

In the tight confines of the Jeep, which he hadn't yet started, he could smell the sweet scent of her shampoo, could see all her smooth, soft skin, could reach out and touch her whenever he wanted, which was only every living second. He was right in thinking it had to stop. Some men might mistake love for lust, but not Chance. He knew that what was happening to his insides, this gut-twisting, brain-boggling need for her was just a major case of lust. That was all. "Ally—"

"Those clouds really do look dark," she said. "It's going to storm. I love the rain."

Yeah, so did he. He could see the two of them, out in the wilderness, the rain pounding over their slick, naked, straining bodies as he brought her to another mind-blowing, screaming, wild climax—

"Chance?" She looked at him then. "Don't ask me to get out."

"Ally—"

"Please? We don't have to talk." A ghost of a smile crossed her face. "Girl Scout's honor."

Thank God.

She let him sink into a comfort zone, let him start the Jeep and get down the curvy mountain road a good mile or so before she said, "But it would be nice."

He nearly crashed. He'd known not to take this...this *thing* between them this far. Only he hadn't listened to his brain, no he'd listened to the part of him that had its *own* agenda, and look where it'd gotten him. In a small truck out in the middle of nowhere with a woman who wanted to discuss the relationship he still hadn't admitted they had.

As if the heavens above found this all very amusing, the wind kicked up to what had to be at least eighty miles an hour. The skies decided to open up, too, and the rain came down in sudden droves. The fog, which hadn't been a problem until now, dropped low, blinding them.

It was as good an excuse as any to concentrate on not getting them killed. On one side of the road was a sheer cliff rising two hundred feet above them. There were many craggly pines that had forced their roots into the rock, jutting out at different angles, as much a part of that mountain as the rock itself. The other side of the road was a sheer drop-off.

"Jo said you train here sometimes," Ally said. "In cliff climbing." She pressed her face to the window and sighed. "That's something I really want to try before I leave."

Before I leave. He was torn between wanting her to leave now and wanting her to leave...never. "Haven't you had enough adventures during your time here?"

"No."

He gripped the steering wheel hard. "You're in over your head, Ally. When are you going to admit that?"

For a long moment, she just looked at him, then without a word turned back to the window.

Good. Great. He'd finally accomplished his goal. She hated him. That was a good thing, he told himself.

Which in no way explained his sense of loss. But then he realized he had a bigger problem and pulled over to the side of the treacherous, deserted two-lane road.

Both of them stared at the large, newly fallen branch blocking their way. With a sigh, Chance pulled out his radio and called the resort. "Got a little problem here on the road," he told Jo. "We'll be later than we thought."

Then he turned to Ally. "Stay here." He pulled rain gear from the back seat.

"Why?"

"Because I can handle it."

A storm gathered in her gaze to match the one outside. "Why should I let you do all the work?"

"So you can stay dry?"

She uttered an entirely uncharacteristic word.

Shocked, he stared at her.

"Didn't know I knew that one, huh?" She said it again, then glared at him, all charged up. "I'm stronger than I look, Chance. I can hike. Bike. Kayak. I can help run a resort. Why, I can even get myself dressed in the morning, so believe me, I can lift a damn branch."

"I didn't mean—"

"And you know what else?" Her eyes flashed. "I can have feelings for you if I want to, whether it makes you break out into hives or not." She untied the sweater from around her waist and angrily stuck her arms into it, determination blaring from every pore.

"That sweater isn't going to stop the rain from soaking you."

She twisted around and reached into the back of his Jeep, grabbing his backup oilskin. "This will."

"It's just a damn branch." He was irritated because she looked so good wearing all that stubborn pride. She looked good wearing his jacket, too, which dwarfed her so much that only her fingertips poked out the sleeves.

She looked good looking at him.

She followed him into the storm as he knew she would. She followed him to the branch, as he knew she would. And she lifted right along side of him, though the wind slashed at them, and they were drenched within seconds.

Lightning lit the sky, and almost immediately came the clap of thunder, far too close for comfort. Suddenly an inconvenient branch in the way became a serious threat.

"Go back to the truck," he shouted as they slowly dragged the heavy branch to the side of the road. "I can get it—"

"We're almost done," she shouted right back, straining along with him.

And that's when he saw it in her eyes. Self-doubt. Fear.

But when he blinked and looked again, both were gone. And suddenly he knew the truth—his little city warrior had faked him out. She wasn't nearly as sure of herself as she wanted him to believe.

He should have known, maybe he'd always known, but that she could put on such a good show, make such an unbelievable go of it, staggered him. "You're doing great," he heard himself say to her.

She went still, then flashed him a smile that took his breath. "Thanks."

He was moving backwards towards the edge of the road, hauling the branch with him. She pushed from the other end, from the middle of the highway. They'd nearly cleared enough room for the Jeep to fit through when a car came roaring up the road.

It was moving far too fast, far too recklessly, and Chance waved and shouted for the driver to slow down.

It didn't.

Tourists, he had time to think in disgust. Stupid tourists who thought the weather was exciting, and the roads infallible and their own driving skills perfect.

"Chance." Ally breathed his name, fear etched on her face. "He's going too fast!"

"Ally, move. *Run.*"

But she stood there in the way, mesmerized in horror.

The driver finally noticed the branch, not to mention both Chance and Ally struggling with it, but Chance knew it was too late, and Ally, still out in the middle of the road, was the vulnerable one. With every ounce of strength he had, he whirled, pulling both the branch—and Ally—with him, whiplashing her toward the side of the road where he stood.

She tumbled hard, landing a few feet from the edge of the cliff on her hands and knees.

The driver slowed, and swerved to the right, but it was too-little-too-late. His tires lost traction and the car lost control. It headed directly for Chance's Jeep, and hit with a sickening crunch.

The car came to an abrupt halt.

The Jeep took the impact, and surged with it, moving, sliding toward the cliff, only feet away from where Ally was still on her hands and knees.

Chance started running, putting himself between

Ally and the moving Jeep, thinking he could stop its movement with one great heave, but thankfully Ally scrambled out of the way. Sure that he could still stop the Jeep, saving the vehicle from going over the side of the cliff, he braced himself and reached out. But the strangest thought went through his head.

He was risking his life for a car.

Only weeks ago he would have done it without thinking. But something was different. *He* was different.

Ally screamed his name. It echoed through the wind and over the rain. He turned toward her to tell her not to worry, that he wasn't going to needlessly risk himself, not now, not when he knew the truth.

He'd changed because of *her*.

"Chaaaance!" She was moving back toward him in slow motion, panic and terror in her eyes, her hands waving as she tried to warn him. Because while he'd stopped with his life-altering realization, while he'd decided to walk away, the Jeep hadn't slowed at all, and as it approached the last few feet before the cliff, as it set itself in a motion that couldn't be stopped, it took him with it.

Right over the edge.

It happened so very slowly that Chance literally saw his life flash before his eyes, just as everyone always claimed. He saw his parents, wild and free in Las Vegas, having the times of their lives.

He should have called them more.

He saw his brothers, Kell and Brandon, both big and tough and strong and disciplined.

And though they'd never been close, he should have called them more, too.

It took a lifetime for the Jeep's momentum to take it past him, down the embankment. He grabbed out blindly, and found purchase in a very hard, very wet, very eager to shred-his-skin-to-bits tree.

He clung to it in slow motion as well, watching the Jeep slide down, watching the rain fall, watching dirt and debris hit him, hurt him, until finally, tired, he closed his eyes.

13

HE'S OKAY, HE'S OKAY, he's okay.

This was Ally's mantra as she crawled to the edge of the embankment where Chance and the Jeep had vanished. When she saw the top of his wet, blond head she nearly collapsed in relief.

He was fifteen feet down, hanging on, his arms straining over his head, to a branch that didn't look sturdy enough to hold him. Ten feet below him, on a ledge, sat the Jeep, looking as if it'd been purposely parked there. "Chance!"

"I'm okay," he said, but he didn't move.

Don't panic, don't panic, don't panic. This became her new mantra as she evaluated the situation.

One, she was in the driving rain, far too close to the edge of a cliff that could give away any second now. Two, she was the only one in the world in any immediate position to help Chance. And three, the pathetic, mousy city girl masquerading as Ms. Carefree had better get it together quickly, because she just realized every bit of strength she'd found over the past month had deserted her. "Hang on!" she called down. She whipped around to squint at the car that had hit the Jeep. The man who'd been driving was running toward her. "Do you have a cell phone?" she yelled.

He nodded and made an abrupt about-face, going back for the phone.

Ally was just peering over the cliff again when another car came ripping up the road, peeling to a stop behind the first car.

Brian and Jo came running.

Ally had never been so happy to see anyone in her life. "Get rope," she told Jo. "Get the guy's cell phone and call 911," she yelled to Brian, and they both ran to help.

A sudden calm determination come over Ally then. Without hesitation, she carefully and slowly went over the side of the cliff. "Chance!" she called, moving down an inch at a time, searching for foot and handholds.

He shook his head as if clearing it, and looked up. There was a cut on his forehead, and mud over most of him. When he saw her coming down after him, he lost whatever color he had left. "Ally, no."

Ten more feet. Nine. She wasn't going to stop now. From above, both Jo and Brian reappeared.

"My God!" Jo cried. "Ally, stop— Wait!"

She couldn't now, she was committed. And halfway there. Brian came over the edge as well, and started his way down to help her.

Again Chance shook his head, looking a little green around the edges. But he was alert, and he reached up to start the climb.

Ally kept moving toward him, heart in her throat. Hand over hand she went, reaching out carefully, trying not to think too hard about what she was doing, because if she did, she'd lose it. She grabbed at a rock, but it came loose, setting off a slide of rocks and debris. With a gasp, she flattened herself against the side of the mountain, cringing as both she and Chance, who had nearly met her now, took several hits.

"Watch out," Jo yelled from above. "Watch out for—"

"I'm okay!" Terrified, but okay. The strenuous climb was taking every bit of concentration she had, so she jerked in surprise when suddenly Chance was at her side. She wanted to cry, wanted to grab him, wanted to shake him and make sure he never ever did anything heroic ever ever again, but he was looking at her with that same look right back and she couldn't speak.

"You don't have a rope on," he said hoarsely, maneuvering sideways so he could curve an arm around her. "Ally, my God, if you let go—"

She both laughed and cried, but didn't dare let go to touch him. "Believe me, I'm not letting go. Now tell me the same."

His eyes were so dark, so intense. "I won't fall."

"Promise." It was inane, but she needed to hear him, needed him to keep looking at her like that, always. "*Promise me*," she repeated tightly.

"Promise." He nudged her back up, refusing to go ahead, staying right behind her, one tensed arm on either side of her legs. Unable to help herself, she kept craning her neck to look back at him. His hands were cut, his every muscle straining with effort but whenever she looked at him he managed a grim smile and urged her along. "I'm okay," he kept saying, but she couldn't believe it. They came upon Brian, who looked Chance over as if he were on Search and Rescue duty before silently and efficiently starting the climb back up as well.

Then they were at the edge, climbing up and over, only to fall to the ground in exhaustion.

Chance went to his knees, weaving once before opening his arms, which Ally dove into without thought, clasping herself to his big, warm, filthy chest. Jo locked her arms around the both of them, and they all dragged Brian into the fray, squeezing hard.

"Okay, so maybe you're ready for rock climbing," Chance quipped, but the smile didn't meet his eyes, which were strained and shadowed.

"That might have been more adventure than I ever planned on," Ally admitted.

"That was too much for anyone." He held her so tight she could barely draw air into her lungs, but breathing came in a distant second to being cradled against him.

He was bigger than life. He was brave and untamed. He was uninhibited and earthy, and his love for the outdoors was contagious.

But she was also madly in love with him and he didn't love her back. He never would. She had to remember that.

"I vote that this was enough training for all of next year," Jo said, trying to laugh, but her eyes filled. She couldn't stop hugging everyone, and Ally knew the feeling.

She didn't want to take her hands off Chance ever again.

Brian, clearly uncomfortable with all the emotion, turned away, but before he could walk, Chance stopped him. "In an emergency, I want to be with you, Slick. You're one tough, sharp thinker. Consider yourself promoted to staff status."

"You said I wasn't old enough."

"Not for ski patrol, but we'll find something. You're official, and as of right now, you're on the payroll. Next time you risk your neck for me, you're damn well going to get paid for it."

Forgetting he didn't like to be touched, forgetting he didn't trust adults and that he was openly crying, Brian hugged Chance, a full-bodied, back-slapping hug between two men who weren't afraid to show how they felt.

"Dammit, stop it," Jo said, swiping her eyes and nose on her sleeve.

Ally found herself back in Chance's arms, back in the place she felt the most alive. And the look in his eyes, the heated intensity, the passion, the longed-for affection...everything she could ever want was there.

Yet it wasn't real.

"Ally—"

"I hear sirens," she said, taking a step back out of his warm embrace, afraid to let him finish. She knew what she *wanted* him to say, but not like this. Not in the heat of the moment, surrounded by chaos. Not when it couldn't last.

The paramedic and rescue unit arrived, as well as

the sheriff, who cited the other driver for reckless driving. Chance was momentarily distracted by the paramedics wanting to treat a few nasty scratches. Then the rescue unit needed a report. Arrangements were made for the Jeep to be hauled back up, and finally, *finally*, the road was cleared and they were free to go.

"Ally." Chance stopped her as she would have gotten into Jo's car, and cupped her cheek in his hand. "You're really okay?"

"Fine." She sank into the car and tried not to give in to the tears she'd been fighting for an hour now.

He followed her in, clearly wondering what was wrong, but she avoided his direct gaze. She had to, or she'd lose it. For so long she'd wanted to see that look in his eyes, had hoped and dreamed for it. Now, in this situation, an emergency, with adrenaline flowing, and thrills aplenty, she had it.

And it wouldn't—couldn't—last.

Soon enough, he'd go back to looking at her as if she was a problem he didn't know what to do with. A problem he wanted to go away. He sat right next to her in Jo's little car, pressing his big body close to hers. She could feel the heat and strength of him, could feel his gaze like a caress.

"It was you," he murmured. "You saved me."

"No." God, not his gratitude on top of everything else. That would make it all the harder to bear. "You would have made it without me." Above all else, he was a survivor.

He stroked her jaw, then turned her to face him, his

'eyes both fierce and tender. "*You* got 911 called, *you* said my name over and over, you kept me alert so I didn't let go. *You* were the one, Ally." He reached for her hands, bringing them up to his mouth, gently kissing the scrapes on her knuckles. Then he hauled her close, until she was tucked up against him, holding her as if she were his entire world.

He was trembling, and she stroked her hands up and down his back. "It's okay," she murmured. "You're fine now."

A rough laugh escaped him, and he squeezed her tighter. "Do you think I care about me? It's you, Ally. It's always been you."

"I'm fine," she whispered.

"I'm glad *you're* fine," he told her. "But I'm a wreck, so hold me, Ms. Fine, and don't let go."

Temporary, she reminded herself ruthlessly. He would only feel this way temporarily.

But at the moment, locked against his hard, warm body, she allowed herself to pretend it could last forever.

JO DROVE TO ALLY'S cabin first, which was a huge relief to Ally, who needed to be alone to regroup. To think. And maybe to wallow, just for a moment.

But Chance got out with her.

"What are you doing?" She sounded panicked, but she needed to be by herself. If he so much as touched her again, if he looked at her with *that* look, the one that told her things he didn't mean for her to know, she'd melt. She'd beg him to hold her again and never let go, to make it real.

He'd get the holding part right, oh he most definitely would. And she'd be lost.

"You should go to your cabin and clean up," she insisted, practically shoving him back into Jo's car.

"I want to clean up, but—" He bent to say something to Jo and Brian, something she couldn't hear.

Jo glanced up at Ally, then nodded. Revving the engine, she drove away.

And left him standing there next to her.

The rain continued to come down, but they were already drenched. Chance was staring at her while she stared at the ground. She could feel his gaze caressing her hair, her face. Then she felt his hand skim her back, so softly it nearly made her cry.

"Remember what you wanted to do before that branch blocked our path?" he asked.

She'd wanted to talk. And she'd nearly goaded him into it, just as she'd goaded him into everything they'd ever done together. Pathetic.

"Do you remember?" he asked again, sounding unusually solemn.

"We were going to the store."

He let out a sound of frustration. "You wanted to talk."

"That was then." Now all she wanted was a pity party, and she was damn entitled. When she was done feeling sorry for herself, she planned to dry herself off and get on with her life. Her heart was broken, but she'd survive.

She always did.

"I think talking is a good idea."

He didn't look as if he thought so. He looked as if he'd offered to face the guillotine. "Your timing is off," she informed him as if she were bored, but he simply slipped an arm around her waist and pulled her into the curve of his body, sheltering her from the rain.

"What are you afraid of?" he asked, mocking her own earlier words.

You. "I just don't feel like talking, Chance."

"Well I do," he said simply, and propelled her inside, out of the rain.

14

FRESH FROM HER SHOWER, Ally paced the kitchen, ignoring the hot chocolate Chance had made her. From the bathroom she could hear the shower running. Then it abruptly turned off.

Chance was in there. Standing in her shower, water streaming down his leanly muscled body. A body that was tough. Hot to the touch. Gorgeous.

And naked.

His hair would be in spikes around his head. He'd probably just shove his fingers through it, as he seemed to do most of the time. His eyes would be tired, his voice deep and husky from the exhaustion of the day. He needed sleep, and she thought maybe he intended to do that here.

If only he knew how she'd fallen so stupidly in love with him, he'd be running for the hills.

As she'd told him, she'd changed.

Actually, both of them had. Where he'd once been unwilling to let anyone into his fiercely guarded, loner heart, he'd opened up and let Brian in. He'd opened up for her as well, as much as he could. That it wasn't enough for her wasn't his fault.

Which meant it was time for *her* to be running for the hills. Or at least for San Francisco.

He'd built a fire, probably to comfort and warm her, but each time it crackled and sizzled she jumped. She left the small kitchen for the living room, hoping the warmth would penetrate her chill.

Chance stood in the doorway, his face dark and pensive. He hadn't bothered to dry his hair and he smelled like her shampoo. When he saw her, he smiled but she noted the tightness of his shoulders and the grimness in his gaze. He was worried, which startled her. She'd seen him in good humor, and in bad. She'd seen him in the throes of passion, and in a foul temper. She'd seen him sad, and also afraid. But never worried.

"I needed you today," he said. "I needed you...and you were there."

She knew all too well this was a problem for him. He made it a point to never need anyone.

"It meant risking your life, and you didn't even hesitate." He shook his head. "I can't stop thinking about that, or about how I felt when I thought that car was going to hit you, right in front of me."

"But it didn't hit me. You made sure of that."

"From the very beginning, when you first came here, I had this ridiculous need to keep you safe." He laughed mirthlessly. "I didn't understand it. And I fought it every step of the way because it drove me crazy watching you do all the things I do every day, all the dangerous things I do and just take for granted because I've done them before. But when *you* did them... God. When *you* went biking, kayaking, *anything*, I had to hold my tongue and...just let you."

"I don't remember you holding your tongue very much," she said wryly.

"My point is that it was pure hell to watch you go at this life with such gusto. It was hell, but I did it, and today—" He drew a deep, ragged breath. "Today it almost cost you your life."

"My life is mine to run," she said softly. "Not yours."

"I know. I'm trying to back off. I know you wanted to be alone now. I know you wanted to pull away from me, and maybe I should have let you." Turning his back to her, he walked to the fireplace and stared pensively into the fire. "But I couldn't."

His shoulders looked as if they were holding the weight of his entire world. Ally had never been able to watch someone in pain and not try to ease it, and there was no way she could hold back here, with him. She crossed the room and slipped her arms around him from behind, laying her cheek against the sleek muscles of his back. Her hands found their way beneath his T-shirt, sliding over the hard sinew and warm skin of his stomach.

At first he didn't move, just stood rock-still so that the only sound was the roaring fire and his own harsh breathing.

Her fingers danced over him, up and down and back again. Then she whispered his name.

It unleashed him, and with a jagged sigh, he turned in her arms, locked his around her, buried his face in her hair, letting out a heartfelt groan. "Ally, I want you. Say you want me, too."

"You know I do."

"Say it."

"I want you, Chance."

His mouth found her neck and nuzzled there, at the sensitive spot beneath her ear, and the embrace changed, shifted into something far more complicated than comfort.

"I want to feel you," he murmured, his hands streaked over her body, cupping, stroking, holding. "I have to feel you."

Again, that thrill, that squeeze on her heart, because he *did* need her. Maybe not on the mountain, but now, right now, and that this big, tough, strong man could be rendered helpless by that need made her want to burst. "Touch me, Chance."

He took her down to her knees on the rug before the fire, removing pieces of clothing as they went. Lying back, he pulled her over him so that she straddled his hips, and it was incredible how he looked up at her, as if she was the most beautiful, most sexy, most amazing woman on earth.

And for that moment, she was. "Touch me," she whispered again.

He reached between them to do just that, his fingers driving her with a deliberate sureness that told her he already knew her body better than she did. "Like this?" he asked, his fingers slipping into her with exquisite care. He brought her to the edge with one stroke. She grabbed his arms so tightly she probably bruised him, but she didn't want him to stop. Not ever.

"Ally?"

"Yes! Yes, like that!" She dipped down and ran the tip of her tongue across his bottom lip. His breath caught, and beneath her, she felt him, hard and heavy, pushing against her soft flesh, felt the thrust of his hips against hers. Fisting him in her hands, she stroked him slowly from base to tip, thrilling to the way his body writhed.

When he couldn't take it any longer, he pushed her hand away. Splaying his fingers over her bare back, he urged her forward, drawing her close so that he could open his lips on one of her breasts. His tongue flicked over her nipples, laving each of them with equal care before drawing one between his lips to suck hard. The pressure continued to build within her and her body tightened. "Now, Chance. Please, now."

Eyes fierce, mouth taut in a line of hunger and need, he guided her over him, sinking into her slowly, so slowly she thought she would die from the wanting. They were naked body pressed to naked body, sweat-slicked skin to sweat-slicked skin, and she couldn't get enough of him, of touching, of tasting him. She couldn't talk, couldn't breathe, couldn't do anything for fear of blinking and having it all be gone. It couldn't be so real, so right...could it? Afraid to let herself hope and dream, she had to close her eyes, had to hide, but he placed his hands on the sides of her face and made her look at him.

"No hiding now." His eyes were alive with passion, his mouth wet from hers, his breathing labored as if he'd run a race. "No more hiding for either of us."

No more hiding. Good thing, because the love she was holding back was currently threatening to choke her. "Chance—"

"Yes. Now. Watch." And he rolled her to her back, surging up so that she could see him enter her with each flex of his hips, could watch her own hips rock up to meet his. It was the most erotic thing she'd ever seen and she struggled to keep her eyes open, to bite off the dark sounds of unbelievable pleasure as she strained against him.

"It's never been like this," she told him. *"Never."*

He stilled for a moment, then plunged deeper, harder, again and again until she started to shudder. Her climax ripped through her, ripping her heart and soul as well. "I love you," she whispered and he shuddered, too, letting out a low, wrenching groan as his own orgasm gripped him. She wondered if he'd heard her words, but the mixture of passion and torment on his face said that he had. Threading his fingers through her hair, he gathered her close for a kiss that claimed her mouth as surely as he'd claimed her heart.

And when they could breathe, he took her again, as if he could somehow drive the need out of him. And then again, deep into the night. Finally, he fell into an exhausted slumber, and for a long, long time Ally watched him sleep, thinking she would give anything to be entwined with him like this forever, held against his chest, close to his heart.

But as soon as he woke up, this special interlude would be over. Oh, she'd let him touch her again, because she couldn't resist. He was a masterful lover.

But she knew now without a doubt what she wanted in life, and it had to be more than lust. As the light of dawn drifted through the slats on her wooden blinds, she touched him one last time, her fingers skimming over his rough jaw, her eyes soaking up every inch of him. "You're so beautiful," she whispered. "Inside and out."

He didn't budge, lost in his exhausted slumber.

"I'll never forget you," she said softly. "Never."

And she slipped out of bed.

WHEN CHANCE WOKE AN hour later, he found himself reaching for Ally. It shocked him, how natural it felt to do so. How natural it felt to look into her big gray eyes and want her to smile at him. He thought about what it would be like to roll over every single morning for the rest of his life and reach for her, and had to admit, he liked the thought.

Where was his usual restlessness after a night like the one they'd shared? Where was his urge to get out of bed and run like hell?

Gone. Vanished, like the rest of his reserve when it came to Ally. He'd never felt this way for another woman. He actually wanted more. He wanted all those things he'd never given much thought to before. Commitment. A home. Children. *Forever.*

But Ally hadn't asked him for any of those things. To the contrary, she'd always planned on leaving. And for the first time in his life he found himself in the awkward position of wanting more from a woman than she wanted from him. Yes, he was completely over the top in love with her, and she loved him back. He might not deserve that love, but she'd offered it and he wanted it more than his next breath.

But she was still leaving.

He lay still for a moment, absorbing that, and the fact she wasn't in the bed with him. She'd come back any second, he told himself, maybe even with that sexy yet shy smile, the one that made him want to tumble her down again and have his way with her.

Which he'd done many satisfying times during the night.

A grin broke free at that, and he stretched languidly, lasciviously, thinking no matter what time it was, they could spare a few extra moments to make love again. Then he'd tell her how he felt about her. It was time to let go of his fear of commitment, time to give in and realize Ally would never hold him back, she'd only enhance everything about his life.

It took him awhile, but he eventually realized the cabin was far too still. He slid his hand over the pillow they'd shared, when she hadn't been sleeping sprawled across the top of him. He'd learned many things about the incredible, warm, passionate Ally in their time together, and one of them was that she was a complete and utter bed hog.

He liked that about her.

But her side of the pillow, though seeped in her light, sexy scent, was ice-cold.

With a jerk of his heart, he shoved up to a sitting position, his gaze searching the room. The closet was open and he pushed the covers aside and hopped out of bed to go look. He tore past the leggings, the new fleece sweats, the wet suit...everything she'd purchased here at the resort. He was looking for the clothes she'd brought with her from San Francisco, the clothes she'd never once worn here, but they were gone.

And so was she.

He threw on his clothes and ran down the path to the lodge. She'd be there, he told himself.

But she wasn't. He searched everywhere, and the longer he searched, the more desperate he became because he knew the ugly truth. He'd made her unhappy. God, what he'd give to fix that. He wanted to see her smile at him with that love in her eyes, the love he'd been afraid of. He wanted to live with her and watch them both turn gray. He wanted every damn thing. But it was too late.

He was too damn late.

All Jo knew was that she'd indeed left. When Chance called Lucy, she was annoyingly vague, too, telling him she was being released in a few days, that she'd come by the resort to see everyone and that they could talk then.

He couldn't wait that long. His heart felt like someone had taken a two-by-four to it. How could he have waited so long to face the truth about loving Ally? He'd been so busy being the big, bad, tough T. J. Chance, only his sweet, determined Ally had really been the brave, tough one all along. She'd gone against the grain just to come here. To stay here. She'd

risked her self-esteem and confidence to face this
world she'd known nothing about.

Over and over again, she'd put herself out on the
line. Learning. Experiencing. *Risking*. And she'd
risked the one thing he never had—his heart.

15

EACH TIME ALLY HAD been to see Lucy, her aunt had seemed fresh, happy and full of spunk. And each time, Ally had left the hospital with a niggling feeling that she was somehow missing something.

Things were no different on this early, foggy morning as she made her way to Lucy's room. She hadn't called first, but *she'd* been the surprised one.

The traction was gone.

In fact, there was no sign of an invalid at all. And though she knew Lucy had been progressing wonderfully, that she was close to being healed, it was still a shock.

As Ally entered the room, Lucy and a nurse were laughing over a joke that the doctor had just told—the doctor that had released Lucy.

Ally stood rooted in the doorway, dividing her gaze between the grinning nurse and Lucy. "You're getting out of here?"

Lucy went utterly still, then plastered a smile on her face. "Darling, how lovely to see you! What a surprise! You shouldn't have driven all this way just to see little, old, rickety me."

"Why do I have the feeling you've never been little, old or rickety?" Suspicious, and feeling as if the joke was on her, Ally moved closer. "How come you didn't let any of us know you were coming home today?"

"Well...I..."

"Lucy, have you been faking all along?"

"No!" She sent her nurse a pleading look. "Tell her. Tell her I was helpless in traction, lying around for days in agony."

"Agony, yes," the nurse said, smiling fondly at Lucy. "Helpless? Never." And with that, she left them alone.

Ally waited for an explanation that didn't seem to be coming. "Lucy?"

"I'm thinking, dear."

"About?"

"How to best approach this."

Ally let out a disbelieving laugh. "How about starting from the beginning? Now, please."

Lucy grimaced. "Are you this tough with your sisters?"

"I am now."

"Well...I guess that's a good thing." Lucy sighed dramatically. "You're not going to like this, you know."

Ally already knew that by the way her heart was drumming. "Try me."

"Okay, well, I really did hurt myself." Lucy slid the sheet aside, revealing the bottom half of her legs, one of which was still in a cast. "See?" She wriggled her purple polished toenails. "Definitely broken."

"Skip to the part I'm not going to like," she suggested tightly.

"You mean where I confess I've been matchmaking this entire time?" Lucy smiled sheepishly, looking twelve instead of sixty something. "Is that the part you mean?"

"You...*what?*"

"I'm sorry."

"But that's—" Ally sank to the bed in shock, the breath swooshing out of her lungs. "How? You didn't even know for certain I'd come here. And you *couldn't* have known that I'd fall for Chance, much less even like him—"

Lucy gasped. Her eyes lit up and she brought her hands to her mouth. "Oh darling! It worked? Really? You fell for him?"

"I..." Even as the trap surrounded her, as the noose tightened, Ally refused to go down without a fight. "I don't know what you're talking about."

Lucy let out a dreamy sigh. "It's too late, I can see it in your eyes."

"That's bad temper!"

"It's love."

"I can't believe this." She felt dazed, railroaded. Mortified. "What a rotten thing to do!"

"Oh, no. No, I didn't mean it that way," Lucy said urgently. "I just thought—"

"What? That it'd be fun to mess with my life?"

"No, of course not. Ally..."

But she didn't want to hear it. Not when the implications of everything were just setting in. She stalked the length of the room to the door, then whirled back. "It was all a ploy? The letter, the job? Everything?"

She waited for the denial that couldn't come because it was all true. "You never really needed me at all."

"No! I—"

"You were bored? You wanted to amuse yourself, and contrived a way to put my *entire* life on hold? Is *that* it?"

"Oh, honey..." Lucy wrung her hands. "This is not going as I planned."

God, she felt so foolish. *Humiliated.* "You played on my sense of family loyalty to get me out here. I can't believe how I fell for it. And all this time I thought I was helping you."

Lucy lifted a hand and pointed at her. "Now you stop right there, Ally Wheeler! True, yes, that's all this family ever does—lean on you. I know that, and it's wrong. I just thought it was time you got something back for once, and I know for a fact you *did* get something back by running Sierra Peak, so don't you tell me otherwise. You learned to trust yourself, you learned just how strong and independent you can be."

Ally sank to a chair and let out a little laugh.

"And you know what else? I think you learned a whole hell of a lot more than that. Not that you'll admit it to me right now, but I think you learned how to *receive* love as well as give it."

Ally stared at her. What would Lucy say if she told her she was right, she'd received lots of "love." On her desk. Against a tree. In the kitchen. The shower... Her heart cracked and broke. "Chance was in on this, right? Give the city girl a thrill?" A man like him would never have given her a second look, why in the world hadn't she seen that? Because she hadn't wanted to, she'd been too busy reacting with her hormones.

"I swear to you, honey. Chance had *nothing* to do with this."

"I need air." Desperate for it, she headed toward the door.

"Dammit—" Lucy fought wildly with her covers, trying to get out of the bed. *"Dammit!"* She flung up her hands in frustration. "If you're going to leave, then help me up so I can follow you. We're not finished!"

Ally stared at the door in front of her, knowing she should walk out, but she couldn't. Miserable, she studied the white paint, but what she really saw was Chance lying sprawled out in her bed, rumpled and sexy from the night they'd spent.

Loving each other.

Her throat tightened. Her eyes burned.

"Ally. Oh, Ally, I'm so sorry."

"Yeah. Me, too," she told the door.

There was more rustling and more swearing. "Then get back here and let me shake you!"

Ally laughed a little, swiped at the silly tear that had escaped, and slowly turned to face her. "Don't hurt yourself. Just stay put."

"Not until you understand—"

"I do. I know that you care about me, and that—"

"I *love* you, dammit. And I *love* Chance. If ever there were two people who deserved to find each other more, I don't know who they are. I just thought—"

"You thought wrong." With a sigh, Ally moved back to the bed. She would not take her pain out on Lucy. "You should know you've been meddling in vain. I came to tell you it's time for me to go. Now that you're getting out of here, the timing is perfect."

"Don't tell me he found someone else, I know that boy too well."

"No, that's not it."

"Good. Now tell me you love him again."

"Lucy—"

"Tell me!"

Ally swallowed hard, but the truth came out. "Okay, fine. You win. I fell in love with him. But—"

Lucy's eyes flared with triumph. "No buts needed."

"*But*, whether Chance loves me back or not doesn't matter." She had to swallow hard. "Not when he doesn't *want* to love me. That's why I have to go. Please understand. If I stay, I'll go weak again. I'll take whatever pathetic scraps of attention he can give me, because I can't resist him. I'll take it and feel grateful for even that little bit."

Lucy's eyes filled. "Oh, honey."

"It's over, Lucy," she whispered. "And I have to leave. I'm sorry."

Lucy reached out a hand, and this time Ally took it. When Lucy tugged and gathered her in for a warm hug, Ally returned it with all her heart.

"I don't want you to go," Lucy murmured. "You've made a place for yourself here. Both in my heart and at the resort, and I know you may not believe this... I hardly believed it myself when I first realized it, but I don't want to work twenty-four/seven anymore." She pulled back to stare into Ally's eyes. "I want to cut back. I want to relax."

Ally shook her head. "Don't you dare add offering me a pity job to your crimes."

"This is *not* a pity job. I swear!" Lucy was vehement. "I would never offer you or *anyone* a job out of pity. I respect hard work too much for that. I just really want to work less. A lot less. And I really thought you were meant for Wyoming. You've got stamina, willpower and a heart of gold." She hugged Ally tight. "So think about it, okay? Think about staying here anyway."

Ally squeezed Lucy tight and fought back more useless tears. "It's ironic, how much I want to stay. How much I've grown to love it here." The mountains, the trees, the silence, the inner peace it gave her...she didn't want to lose it.

"Then stay."

Ally closed her eyes. "I can't." Her entire life was in front of her. Surely she could do something with it, something worthwhile. "Besides, I have to go close out my apartment. The building was sold before I even came here."

"I know." Lucy pulled back, looking innocent. *Too* innocent. "Who do you think bought it?"

Ally laughed in disbelief. *"No."*

"Yes."

"But the cost... I didn't think you had—"

"Oh, I have the money. And before you ask, I've been trying to help your parents for years, but they have such pride, Ally. They're wonderful people."

Ally smiled fondly. "I know."

"And you're wonderful, too. I just wanted to pay you back for all you've ever done in the name of family loyalty."

"You already have."

"No, I could never do that, you've given so much. Go, honey. I know you think you have to. But I'll make you a little hopeful wager. That you'll be back."

"Don't count on it," Ally warned.

"Oh, but I will. You need to go back and see how little that city really means to you. Then you'll come back. Back where you belong."

"No." Ally couldn't. She couldn't face seeing Chance every single day. "I'm sorry, Lucy."

Lucy refused to hear it. "Make it a quick trip. I'm thinking about learning how to hang-glide."

When Ally's jaw dropped, Lucy hugged her again and laughed. "Just kidding."

Ally wasn't so sure.

TWO TERMINALLY LONG days later, Ally had nearly finished packing up her apartment, with a few days to spare on her lease.

Not that *that* mattered now, she thought with a renewed sense of amazement at how far Lucy had gone to get her to Wyoming. Thanks to Lucy, she didn't have to rush, and she hadn't yet decided on another place.

Exhausted but pleased with her progress, she sat on the floor, surrounded by a sea of boxes, all in various stages of packing.

And she yearned for Chance.

Outside her tiny window, cars honked, a plane buzzed by, a siren screamed...city sounds. She hadn't slept well because of the noise, not when she'd gotten so used to the quiet and peaceful wilderness.

She wanted that soul-fortifying silence back.

And if she wanted a lot more than that, if she wanted warm, loving arms to hold her at night, if she wanted those arms to belong to T. J. Chance, then she could put that in the back of her mind.

He wasn't that type of guy. Forever wasn't his thing.

No matter that it had become hers.

She hadn't slept a wink since she'd left, not because of the stupid city noises, not out of worry of closing up her apartment, but because she missed him.

She missed the way he saw so much joy in everything outdoors, and the way he made her see it, too. She missed his laugh, and how he made *her* laugh. She missed his touch. Only with him did she feel like a woman capable of bringing a man to his knees with a simple kiss. It was a power she relished, and wanted to feel again.

But most of all, she missed the way she felt when she was with him. Alive. As if she could do anything.

The knock at her door startled her. So did the achingly familiar male voice. "Ally."

It'd been days since she'd heard him, and hearing him now rendered her a trembling, yearning wreck.

He knocked again, less politely. "Ally, open up."

Before she could even rise to her feet, he helped

himself. In he came, larger than life, looking as if he'd just strode in from off the mountain. His hair was windblown, his bare arms and face tanned and rugged. He wore jeans and a T-shirt, his standard uniform, and just looking at him brought an ache of loneliness to her chest.

When he saw her sitting on the floor, he dropped his small duffel bag and strode toward her. Each step he took caused her heart rate to double. *Triple.*

The boxes in his way were shoved aside, his dark and intense gaze never wavering from her face. "I have some questions for you," he said.

It was hard to be casual with her heart in her throat. "I would have thought Lucy had covered any problems."

He faltered, looking shocked. And...hurt? "You think I'm talking about the resort?" But before she could so much as blink, he hauled her up, her toes dangling off the floor, nose to nose with him, and gave her a light shake. "You think I flew all the way out here to ask you about the *job* you left?"

"Well, I—"

"You left my bed without a word," he grounded out. "You left my *life* without a word."

"Actually, it was *my* bed."

He looked almost baffled, as if no one had every walked away from him before. "You were with me. In my arms. Soft and sated and glowing from what I thought was one of the best nights of my life."

"It was," she agreed, and completely upended his temper by laying her hand along his jaw. "It was."

He resisted the urge to bury his face in her hair and beg her to come back, because he knew what he'd done wrong, knew how he'd lost her. Oh yeah, he knew exactly. And he had to face it, quite possibly making this the biggest adventure he'd ever been on. "You just vanished," he whispered. "Just took your stuff and...left. Lucy was no help, she just told me I was an idiot and I'd figure it all out in good time, whatever the hell that means. Dammit, why didn't you tell me you were leaving?" But he couldn't bear it, couldn't handle hearing he'd gotten only what he deserved—his solitude, which was what he'd always wanted before Ally. So he covered her mouth with his and kissed her for all he was worth. He kissed her and kissed her, heart roaring, body quaking, because given that he'd found her packing for who-knows-where, he might have missed her entirely.

He might have never seen her again.

"If I'd known you were going to leave town," he vowed hoarsely, spreading openmouthed kisses along her jaw. "I would have...I could have—"

She went still, and pulled back to look at him. "What, Chance? You would have what?"

Words failed him. They always had around her. Instead, he banded his arms around her, kicked some boxes out of his way and backed her to the couch, where he dumped her.

Her little shriek was muffled because he followed her down, bridging her body with his own. Looking into her surprised face, he started working on the buttons of her blouse.

"Chance!"

"You left because you don't have any feelings for me?"

Her eyes widened and, duly sidetracked, her fingers left the material of her blouse to cup his face. "You know I have feelings for you."

"I've always considered myself pretty tough, you know." He undid another button, revealing the clasp on her lacy bra and the inside curves of her breasts, the sight of which made him dizzy. "Not needing anyone or anything. Never have—" Another button, and he looked into her face. "And I was sure I never would." The last button came away. "But then you sauntered into my life, Ally, all sweet and giving and warm... irresistible." Slowly, he parted her blouse. His stomach clenched at the glorious sight of her breasts, straining against the lace with each breath she drew.

"Chance." She put her hands over his. "This is crazy."

"I know. I know your family leans on you too much, and I promise, Ally, I promise never to do that to you. You'll never have to give up anything to care about me."

She opened her mouth and he set a finger to her lips. "You changed me," he told her as he stroked a finger down her neck, between her breasts, over her belly to play with the hook on her shorts. He leaned in close to slide his jaw over hers. "And I figured it out after you left me. You were the brave one all along, did you know that? You risked heart and soul, over and over, while I kept everything safe and sound, tucked deep inside."

"Oh, Chance."

"Some big, bad adventurer, huh? I have feelings for you." His voice was unsteady as he fingered the lace on her bra, the creaminess of her skin. In reaction, her nipples hardened, pressed against the lace, making him tremble like a damn baby. He slid his thumb over a jutting peak, loving the sound that ripped from her throat. "You make me happy," he told her. "In a way I've never been before."

She gripped his arms tightly, as if she desperately needed the balance. "I make you...happy?"

"Oh, yeah." He opened her bra, then skimmed both it and her shirt over her shoulders. "My head spins just thinking about you. It scared the hell out of me at first," he admitted, filling his eyes with the feast of her as he went back to concentrating on her shorts.

"Chance—" Again she put her hands on his. "What are you doing? What are *we* doing?"

Surging up, he pulled his shirt off and tossed it across the room, going hot when she stared at him hungrily. "We're getting naked." He removed the rest of their clothing, leaving her sprawled beneath him wearing only a nervous expression. He stared deep into her eyes. "You left me, and I know why. It's because, by some miracle, you fell in love with me."

She looked away at that, pain flickering in her gaze, and he cupped her face and brought her back. "I denied my feelings for you, and in doing so, I hurt you. I'll never forgive myself for that, but I can promise you, I'll never do it again. I need you in my life." He drew in a badly needed breath. "I love you, Ally." His smile wobbled. "I've never said those words to a woman before, other than Lucy."

Her smile was no less wobbly. "So why now?"

"Because I don't want to be without you. I can be with or without the resort, even with or without Wyoming, but God, Ally, agree to be mine, because it's *you* I can't be without."

"This is a really cruel dream."

"You're not dreaming." She hadn't said she loved him and he was dying. He blew out a harsh breath and dropped his forehead to hers. "Ally, it's real. Marry me."

"But you don't want to give up your freedom."

"I'd give up my last breath to have you."

Her eyes filled, but she just stared at him.

"You know you're killing me here, right? God, Ally, say something. Say yes."

She threaded her fingers through his hair and pulled him close enough that their mouths brushed. "Yes."

His breath deserted him. He could hardly talk. "Yes to which?"

"To everything." She both laughed and cried. "Yes, I love you. Yes, oh most definitely *yes*, I want to marry you."

"Here?" She didn't know it yet, but he didn't intend to ever let her go. "How about now?"

She smiled, and though it was a bit wet, it was the

most beautiful smile he'd ever seen. "I want to marry you in Wyoming."

The band around his chest loosened only slightly, but his eyes stung with burning hope and love. "You'll come back?"

"I never left, not in spirit anyway. It's in my heart. It's my home," she said simply. She touched his face. "I told Lucy where I'd gone. I thought maybe she'd tell you."

He shook his head. "The damn meddling woman. If I hadn't seen her fall off that bike with my own eyes, I might think she set me up."

"Well..." Ally laughed. "Not with the broken bones, but she did set you up. She set both of us up. Literally."

His eyes widened. "You're kidding me."

"Sneaky of her, I agree, but effective." She danced her fingers down over his bare chest, and was rewarded when his breathing quickened and his eyes darkened. "It brought you here to me. Tell me again, Chance."

"I love you. I always will."

"Now show me," she demanded.

He was on his way to doing just that, and had them both halfway to bliss, when she smiled, her entire heart in her gaze, and said, "I hope we're making a baby."

It was a good thing he wasn't standing. His knees went weak and his heart soared. "A girl," he managed. "With your stormy eyes and brave heart."

"And her daddy's sense of adventure."

"Sounds good," he murmured huskily, bending close for a long, deep, hot kiss. "Now where were we?"

"Oh dear, I've lost track." Her grin was wicked. "Better start at the beginning."

"Perfect. I love beginnings."

MAITLAND MATERNITY

Where the luckiest babies are born!

In April 2001, look for

HER BEST FRIEND'S BABY

by Vicki Lewis Thompson

A car accident leaves surrogate mother Mary-Jane Potter's baby-to-be without a mother—

and causes the father, Morgan Tate, to fuss over a very pregnant Mary-Jane like a mother hen. Suddenly, Mary-Jane is dreaming of keeping the baby…and the father!

Each book tells a different story about the world-renowned Maitland Maternity Clinic— where romances are born, secrets are revealed… and bundles of joy are delivered.

Where love comes alive™

Visit us at www.eHarlequin.com

MMCNM-8

Finding Home

New York Times bestselling authors

Linda Howard
Elizabeth Lowell
Kasey Michaels

invite you on
the journey of a lifetime.

**Three women are searching—
each wants a place to belong,
a man to care for her,
a child to love.**

Will her wishes be fulfilled?

*Coming in April 2001
only from Silhouette Books!*

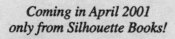

Silhouette®
Where love comes alive™

Visit Silhouette at www.eHarlequin.com   PSHOME

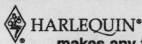

INDULGE IN A QUIET MOMENT
WITH HARLEQUIN

Get a FREE
Quiet Moments Bath Spa

with just two proofs of purchase from
any of our four special collector's editions in May.

**Harlequin® is sure to make your time special this Mother's Day
with four special collector's editions featuring a short story
PLUS a complete novel packaged together in one volume!**

Collection #1   Intrigue abounds in a collection featuring *New York Times* bestselling author Barbara Delinsky and Kelsey Roberts.

Collection #2   Relationships? Weddings? Children? = *New York Times* bestselling author Debbie Macomber and Tara Taylor Quinn at their best!

Collection #3   Escape to the past with *New York Times* bestselling author Heather Graham and Gayle Wilson.

Collection #4   Go West! With *New York Times* bestselling author Joan Johnston and Vicki Lewis Thompson!

Plus Special Consumer Campaign!
Each of these four collector's editions will feature a
"FREE QUIET MOMENTS BATH SPA" offer.
See inside book in May for details.

Only from
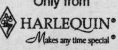
HARLEQUIN®
Makes any time special ®

Don't miss out! Look for this exciting promotion on sale in May 2001,
at your favorite retail outlet.

Visit us at www.eHarlequin.com   PHNCP01